Monsters In Her Head

The Monsters You Know
Book Two

Erin Bedford

Cover Design by Atlantis Book Designs

Proofing by Makenzie Frazier

Editing by Jaime Gardner

Also by Erin Bedford

The Underground Series

Chasing Rabbits
Chasing Cats
Chasing Princes
Chasing Shadows
Chasing Hearts

The Crimes of Alice

The Crimes of Alice
Hatter's Heart
Cheshire's Smile

The Mary Wiles Chronicles

Marked by Hell
Bound by Hell
Deceived by Hell
Tempted by Hell
Betrayed by Hell

Her Angels

Heaven's Embrace
Heaven's A Beach
Heaven's Most Wanted

Fairy Tale Bad Boys

Beauty and the Hunter
Wendy's Pirate
More Precious Than Gold
Mirror
Stepbrother

Starcrossed Dragons

Riding Lightning
Grinding Frost
Swallowing Fire
Pounding Earth

Curse of the Fairy Tales

Rapunzel Untamed
Rapunzel Unveiled
Rapunzel Unchained

Wicked Crown

Little Morning Star
When Hell Freezes Over
To Hell With It

House of Van Helsing

Her Cross To Bear
Blood Betrayal

House of Durand

Indebted to the Vampires
Wanted by the Vampires
Protected by the Vampires
Embrace of the Vampires
Tempted by the Butler
Loved by the Vampires
Huntress of the Vampires
Judged by the Vampires
Imprisoned by the Vampires

Academy of Witches

Witching On A Star
As You Witch
Witch You Were Here
Just Witch It
Summer Witchin'

Children of the Fallen

Death In Her Eyes
Fire In Her Blood

The Beast of the Fae Court
Granting Her Wish
Vampire CEO

Content Warning

This is a dark fantasy romance and has elements that may be triggering for some individuals, including the sexual and physical abuse of a disabled person.

Read at your own discretion.

Monsters In Her Head

The Monsters You Know

Book 2

Erin Bedford

Chapter 1

THERE WERE WORSE things in this life than to be stuck under a mountain with what most believed were savage monsters. Being engaged to a raging sadist was higher on my list, and one that I planned on never having to follow through with. At least, under the mountain I wasn't subjected to my fiancé's abuse. I only had amorous drakes to worry about.

A little shiver ran down my back at the thought. Contrary to what I had believed, there were actually parts of Mount Boyon that were warmer than others.

The drakes with their half-dragon side didn't notice the cold as much as we full humans did. I'd said as much, and Tat, my faithful drake guard, eagerly showed me this hallway near an underground hot spring. We'd spent many days there in the hallway much to Aryn's and the drake king's displeasure.

"No... that's not right." I threw my head back and laughed at Tat's attempt to sign. I waved his hands down and showed him the correct way. "Fingers like this... and then you tap them together like that."

Tat repeated the hand gesture for "meet you" once more.

"Perfect." I clapped my hands together and smiled at him, while my hands signed my words at the same time.

I'd gotten into the habit since Tat had asked me to teach him how to talk to me like Aryn, my handmaiden, and I did. At first, I was hesitant. I, for sure, thought it could be some kind of trick from Ryu to intrude into my and Aryn's little world. The drake king couldn't handle not knowing everything I said or thought.

Not that he was talking to me right now anyway. Ryu was still mad at me for withholding my true reason for coming to him.

I didn't know why I cared.

Back home, once I lost my hearing, everyone made the effort to learn how to sign so they could interact with me. I was horribly childish and reluctant to learn at first. I didn't want anyone to treat me differently, like I was broken.

Except... I had been. Physically and spiritually. I'd overcome the sickness but lost my mother and my hearing in the process. At that time, I didn't know which one had been worse. After losing my mother, I knew losing my hearing wasn't the worst thing in the world.

I'd give up all my senses to have my mother back in my life again. To have her arms around me, her fingers smoothing over my hair while she sang in my ear. Having her here was far better than not being able to hear anyone's obnoxious voice again.

Unfortunately, I'd learned there were worse things to lose, some of them not measurable by any cleric or shaman. They weren't things most people would even notice until they were taken away.

Dignity. Pride. A sense of self.

Callahan had taken all of those from me, and I would do anything to get them back.

"Nice to meet you," Tat tried again, dragging me out of my thoughts. "What did I say before?" His silver scales glinted in the torch light, the horns on his head standing out more in the little light we had to see by.

"You basically said it was nice to have sex with me." I explained, showing him the signs as I spoke. Tat's eyes widened alone with my smile. "It's easy to get the two mixed up. I just wouldn't say that to Aryn unless you want to get smacked."

Tat rubbed a hand over his face and shook his head. "I think I'll hold off on signing with Aryn. She scares me."

Giggling, I shoved Tat with a hand. Not that the massive drake moved at all. Why were all the drakes so big? I didn't know how they could all fit under this mountain without anyone knowing.

A dark shadow covered us, and Tat scrambled to his feet. I glanced up from the large golden scaled feet to the thick calves and muscular thighs, lingering on the cloth covered waist far longer than I should have before sliding up the hard ridges of the abs I had an overwhelming need to lick. Eventually, I settled on the sharp chin and pillowy lips. The scar bisecting the pale-yellow eye only added to the appeal of the king's brother, Ira.

Unlike Tat, I didn't scramble to my feet so I could then prostrate myself before the drake prince. I simply tipped my head to the side and blinked at him.

His lips moved in small, unreadable movements. Whatever

he said made Tat stiffen and avoid looking at me.

That wouldn't do.

I lifted my hand up to Tat, who immediately grabbed it and helped me to my feet. Ira's lips moved again, and Tat released me abruptly after I straightened completely.

I shot a scowl at Tat before gesturing to him with my hands.

"You left your spine on the ground."

Tat's brows furrowed and then they shot up as he deciphered what I signed. His lips twitched, then flattened just as quickly. He turned on his heel without so much as a flick of his wrist, his tail wagging behind him happily.

Pursing my lips, I turned my ire onto the drake prince before me.

"What did you say to him?"

Ira blinked his good eye at me. Not saying anything, he pivoted away from me and walked away, his long red-orange hair brushing his back as he went.

Scowling at the prince's back, I hesitated for a second before stalking after him. Ira didn't bother to communicate with me as I walked beside him. His good eye slid over to me before moving back to the front.

We walked for a few moments like that, a few drakes passing by every now and again, their eyes sliding to me before jerking away after Ira glared at them. When we reached a tunnel with more torch light than the others, I grabbed Ira by the wrist, his spiked bracelet just inches from stabbing my hand.

"Enough with the mysterious drake act. What did you say to Tat? Where are we going?" I spoke and signed at the same time, though why I did it when Ira couldn't understand my hand signs, I don't know. I supposed my new habit had fully formed now.

Ira's eyes darted from my lips to my hands every few words. His lips ticked up on the unscarred side. This time he actually moved his lips with enough precision that I could understand what he was saying.

"That guard needs to learn his place. You are not friends."

I frowned, crossing my arms over my chest causing the material of the dress I wore to tighten over my form, something Ira's good eye didn't miss. "You don't get to tell me who I am friends with." I smacked my hands together hard enough to sting my hands, making Ira's eyes jerk up to mine again. "You don't own me."

Ira crowded me, forcing me to step back until my back hit the wall of the tunnel. My traitorous body tingled and heated at his proximity, half of me wanting him closer and the other telling me to push him away. The sharp points of his knee guard poked into the soft parts of my thighs. Ira's hand wrapped around my throat, the tip of the claws pinching my skin.

Amusement glittered in his one good yellow eye, his face shoving into my hair breathing me in as his words tickled my mind.

My brother has claimed you. Thus, you belong to the drakes.

It took me a moment to think about what he actually said to me, his warm body against my cooler one distracting me. When I shook myself out of it long enough to understand, I gaped and pushed at his chest.

He didn't budge.

Fucking does not count as claiming. Or I'd have been claimed a long time ago.

Ira's hot breath brushed against my skin, while the claws on his other hand took liberties caressing me through the silky crimson material clinging to my body.

I have no doubt about that. However, since you have offered yourself in exchange for our help against your fiancé, I think the matter is rather moot, wouldn't you?

Anger burned into me. I threw my knee up between Ira's legs. I clearly caught the hardened warrior off-guard, because the blow hit home. The hand on my throat loosened, and I shoved with all my might. Ira stumbled back a few steps.

Baring my teeth at the drake, I shoved myself forward until we were nose to nose. Unlike Ryu, Ira and I were almost the same height. It was much easier to intimidate someone when you could look them in the eye. As I glared, I practically yelled my thoughts at him.

That does not mean you can tell me who I can or cannot spend time with. I will fuck your brother. He will help me get rid of Callahan and Luis. And you, I shoved his chest to no avail, *will treat me with respect.*

Ira's lips curved up to the side as his hand shot out quick as lightning. Before I could move, he'd wrapped my braid around his fist until I was forced to tilt my head back or have my neck break.

I don't think you want me to treat you with respect, princess. He dipped his head and brushed his nose along the side of my exposed throat before lifting his head so I could see his face. *In fact, I think you want someone to treat you like the broken little bird that you are.*

I swallowed thickly against the hammering in my heart. *You don't know anything about me.*

Ira tugged my hair just enough to make me wince before releasing it, his lips moving slowly so I could read them.

"Oh, princess. Believe me, I do. I've been broken too." He pointed at the milky yellow eye and the scar that split it in two jagged lines down his face. "They won't ever know how it feels. The helplessness. The feeling of not being quite whole. Not like us." He played with my braid as my chest heaved up and down against my will.

Let me know when you're ready to give in.

Just as quickly as he had cornered me, Ira strode away, gone before I could retort, leaving me in the hall with my raging heart and throbbing between my thighs.

What was wrong with me?

I realized a few moments later that Ira hadn't told me where we were going. Worse, he'd left me in a part of the mountain I didn't recognize. Before I could panic about getting lost, Beautine appeared around the corner with a bright smile on her pale honey colored face, her fangs peeking out between her lips. The female drake had been a life saver since Aryn and I had come to the drakes hide out. Not only helping us understand the drake's social standings but just in being someone in their court when faced against the other female drakes.

"There you are," I read on Beautine's lips. "I worried that brute of a prince had led you astray. Now," she peered over my form and pursed her lips, "this won't do. You're going to need battle leathers, and I'm thinking you'd do well with daggers. But we will see how you pan out. You never know, you might be a sword or bow kind of person."

I blinked at her. My mind was barely able to keep up with her words.

"What? Why would I need daggers? Or any weapon, for that matter?"

Beautine patted me on the shoulder with a patient smile. "To train, of course. You didn't think we'd just fight your battles for you, did you?"

It seemed everyone had found out about the episode I had with their king a few days ago. Bowing down to the drake king, pleading for his assistance to save my people as well as his own had been the most humiliating thing I'd ever done.

One would think what had happened a few minutes before that would have taken first place. Who cared about my problems when there was juicy gossip to pass around?

But no.

When I thought about the way the drake king had chased me down and then fucked me not only with his bumpy yet massive cock, but I'd also let him shove his tail in my... ugh...

I couldn't even think about it. It made my face and body heat in two entirely different ways. Not that I would let him know that.

Beautine squeezed my shoulder to grab my attention.

"Are you ready?"

Yes. Not for training, for something else entirely. To Beautine, I bobbed my head.

"Lead the way."

Chapter 2
Ryu

RYU'S GAZE BORED holes into the map in front of him. There was the Caffew kingdom to the east. The Gunni to the north. The Haidori to the west. And then there was the kingdom belonging to the princess's betrothed to the south, Plumus. If not for a small tip of Kinoko, Georgia's homeland, touching the ocean, they would be landlocked and have no way out if all four sides attacked at once.

The Kinoko kingdom had a tenuous relationship with the others ever since their queen died. It did not surprise Ryu that one of them jumped at the chance to take over, even if it was through marriage. In fact, he'd expected it to occur sooner than it had.

Ryu growled low in his throat.

Georgia's marriage to Callahan would never happen if the drake king had anything to say about it. Just thinking about the scars on her skin from that sadist made his inner flame burn hot enough to melt steel.

"Woah," his brother, Desmond, whistled, his eyes on Ryu's hands. "Someone is in a mood."

Glancing down, Ryu huffed a sigh at the stone table before lifting his hands. Two melted handprints remained behind as evidence of his rage. Ryu turned his attention back to the map.

"What do you want?"

"Just wanting to check on my older brother." Desmond rounded the table, his gaze moving over the wooden figurines they'd made to represent the different kingdoms' armies. "You did, after all, put us smack dab in the middle of a war, all for some great pussy."

Before Ryu knew what he was doing, he had his brother pinned to the table, a dagger pressed to the younger brother's throat.

Desmond chuckled, not at all bothered by Ryu's outburst. "Touchy subject. Guess it was better than great."

Ryu snarled in Desmond's face, his fangs close to his cheek. "Do not speak about her in such a manner. In fact, do not speak of her at all."

Ryu released his brother with a shove, stabbing his dagger into the table instead. Straightening himself, Desmond rubbed his throat and eyed the map.

"So, do you have any plans for us, oh great king?"

Ignoring his brother's mocking tone, Desmond just wanted to get under his skin, Ryu gestured at the map.

"We need to figure out the numbers we are up against. The princess could only tell me what forces her father has and what soldiers she knows about that her fiancé," the word tasted like poison in his mouth, "has in the palace. However, the scum could have hidden forces all over Kinoko without anyone knowing."

"And what of allies?" Desmond asked, all teasing gone from his face and voice. This was the voice of the general of Ryu's army. "Do you think we can face the force of Plumus alone?"

Ryu shook his head and swiped a hand over one of his horns. "I will not pretend to know what we are up against. But we cannot stand on the sidelines and let the Plumus bastards take over Kinoko, not while we live here as well."

Desmond didn't speak for a long .moment "You know, it has been a while since we moved," he casually commented at last. "We could —"

"No," Ryu snarled at him.

"I'm just saying, it would be smarter for our people to leave Kinoko and Plumus to fight amongst themselves. It is not our battle."

Ryu threw his dagger across the room, aiming for Desmond's head. Desmond ducked and arched a brow at him.

"I'll take that as a no?"

"We are not leaving them to their fate. The others only ostracized them because of the Kinoko protected us. Had they driven us out the moment we made ourselves known, the other kingdoms would not have targeted them so heavily after the queen's death."

Shaking his head, Desmond walked over to the wall and pulled the dagger out.

"You don't know that. It could have happened with or without us being here."

"Regardless, we cannot ignore a request for aid from our hosting kingdom." Ryu shook his head. "If things turn around in their favor and we deny them," he dragged a hand over his face, "that would only be more problems on the horizon."

"Not to mention, the princess would cut off your access to her delectable body."

Ryu shot a scowl at his brother but didn't comment.

The feel of the princess's tight pussy wrapped around his hard length was something Ryu dreamed about. She had taken him so well, moaning and screaming out for all the world to hear her. It wasn't something he was likely to forget soon.

Unfortunately, the princess had withdrawn from him once she achieved his assurance that he would help her. Not that Ryu had tried to push the issue. He wasn't sure he was ready to forgive and forget the lies the princess had told him. His cock had other thoughts, though. He would have to remedy this schism between his head and his dick soon enough.

Desmond blessedly pulled him from his thoughts, where his cock already started to make the argument for forgiving Georgia for her deception.

"And what of the soldiers that showed up in the clearing?"

"What of them?" Ryu shifted a few wooden figurines on the map.

"Will they keep their mouths shut about our location?" Desmond picked up a figurine, swaying it back and forth. "Or do we need to worry about the Plumus prince coming for his princess?"

"No." Ryu shook his head. "They are sworn to the princess and the kingdom of Kinoko. It is in their best interest to keep our location a secret, at least until we resolve the matter of the Plumus cunts."

Desmond snorted and laughed. "That prince sure pulls at your tail, doesn't he?"

Flicking his eyes up from the map to meet his brother's gaze, Ryu glowered. "You would too if you had seen what he'd done to her. No one should treat their females in that manner, least of all one's own future mate."

Desmond bobbed his head in agreement and then, after a moment, tilted his head to the side and clicked his tongue.

"So... what's going to happen once we win?"

Ryu stared down at the map. "What do you mean?"

"Say we fight the Plumus and save the day. What happens then? Do we go back to hiding? Does the princess get to go home? Or do we all just pretend like none of this ever happened?"

The more questions Desmond asked, the more Ryu's chest tightened, a low growl building up in it.

The very thought of sending the princess away, of pretending like none of this happened, was something Ryu couldn't even process it. The only thing he knew for certain was that he wanted the princess. In his bed, beneath him, on top of him, against the wall, in the bath... wherever he could get her. He had not had his fill of her yet and until that was done, he would not let her go.

"Ryu?" Desmond prodded.

"We will figure it out when the time comes," Ryu grunted in answer. He shifted away from the map and stalked toward the door.

"Where are you going?" Desmond called after him.

Ryu didn't bother to answer his brother. His mind was firmly set on finding the princess who had brought all this destruction to his doorstep and turmoil in his body and mind. It was time she started fulfilling her part of this bargain...

Beginning with that sharp mouth of hers wrapped around his cock.

Chapter 3

LEANING BACK AGAINST the side of the hot springs, I groaned.

Beautine had trained me until I dropped and then some. Now I wished I'd taken up sword fighting lessons as a girl when my father offered it to me. Back then I was too into parties and pretty things like my mother. Now, it was biting me in the ass.

Oh, by the gods, my body hasn't ached this much since...

My face heated thinking of the way the drake king had thoroughly fucked not just my pussy but my ass as well. It wasn't as if I'd never had a cock in there before... However, at the same time? I hadn't even realized such a thing was possible or done until Ryu had done it, and a delightfully filthy part of me was dying to do it again.

If only I could push down my pride enough to face him. We'd fucked quiet savagely in the clearing before the guards from my kingdom interrupted us. After that, we'd been silent on our way back inside. Ryu had left me at his bedroom door and went off to do... well, whatever one does to plan a war.

I sat around, waiting for him to come back. When he didn't, I ventured off to find Aryn and explained what had happened. I had hoped when Ryu came to bed that night, he would pick up where we left off, or at least, make some kind of move that he wanted me again.

Unfortunately, I fell asleep before he came back, and then he was gone when I woke up. The only reason I knew he'd been there at all was the hot spot on the bed beside me.

How long would Ryu stay mad at me? Should I try to make peace with him? How would I even go about doing that?

"Sorry I lied to you so I could make you fall in love with my feminine wiles all so you would fight my battles for me?"

I was confident in my skills, but this one was unlikely.

The water shifted around me. I didn't open my eyes, expecting it to be Beautine.

Wanting to know if Beautine had any remedies to help sore muscles, I slit my eyes open slightly. But there was no friendly female drake. There was only the drake king lounging against the other side, his hot gaze boring into my exposed flesh.

My eyes widened, and I ducked further into the water until only my head was visible.

Ryu's lips ticked up. *Shy now, pet?*

I scowled at him. *Don't call me that.*

Snaking through the water, Ryu stopped inches from me. While he didn't touch me, I could feel the heat coming off him, even through the warm water.

Then what should I call you? Love? Little one? Mine?

My face burned with each pet name he offered. I hated to admit it, but all of those made my insides quiver with need. Forcing myself to meet his gaze, I schooled my features into a bored expression.

Princess or Your Highness will do.

Except I outrank you. Should you not be the one lowering yourself to me? Ryu stared at my lips until I caught on to what he meant.

I pushed back in the spring, water sluicing around me as I scrambled to get some distance between us.

I wouldn't say you outrank me. You are only the king of the drakes, and you have no kingdom. This is my land, not yours.

Ryu's lip curved up to show a fang before he was on me in a snap.

My back pressed into the stone of the hot spring as Ryu shoved between my legs, his long hard length pushed up against my throbbing heat. I let out a whimper, desire coursing through me even as his sharp claws hovered inches from my jugular. I grasped the stones behind me to keep myself from grabbing him.

What was that, princess? Ryu's other hand grasped behind my thigh, pulling it over his waist. His tail held my leg there at the calf while he thrust against my core. *I think your body says differently.*

Forcing my brain to get past the lustful fog, I glared up at him. *Involuntary reaction. It would happen with anyone. You're not special.*

Ryu threw his head back and laughed. It rumbled through his chest and vibrated on my nipples making them harden and ache with need.

I would agree with you there. I'm not special. I'm not nice. I'm not a prince who will sweep you off your feet.

His hand cupped my breast, and his thumb brushed my nipple before pinching it until I hissed with a mixture of pain and pleasure.

You knew what you were getting into when you came into my home and offered yourself to me.

Ryu lifted my face up so I could read his lips. "Now, I'm going to take what's mine."

Without warning, Ryu shifted his hips and slammed into me. My back arched up off the stone, my hands scrambling for his shoulders. My nails dug into his scaled back and torso as my hips jerked up with each thrust of his hips, pounding into me so hard that my back scraped against the stone.

His nostrils flared, probably scenting the blood from those scrapes, and he whipped me around. The drake king pulled me into his lap, his hands coming around me to hold me close.

Done fighting it, I grabbed for anything I could hold on to, which ended up being the horns on his head. Ryu became animalistic in his fucking, his hands, his tail, his tongue. Everything was everywhere and all at once, overwhelming me with each touch and flick until I was breaking apart on his cock, my throat going raw from screaming out.

The drake king stilled, his claws tightening on my hips as he held me to him while his hot cum filled me. For a brief moment of clarity, I worried that he might get me pregnant.

The contraceptive potion I usually took for such things was back at home, and I was due to take it in a few days. I'd been sure to take it as soon as Callahan showed up. If the bastard ever tried to take me against my will, I didn't want to end up with a little monster like him bound to me forever.

Ryu lifted my chin, licking his long-forked tongue along my lips and chin. That clarity continued to take hold as I tried to shift out of his lap. That only made him tighten his hold on me further.

I scowled at him. *You got what you wanted. Let me go.*

Amusement sparkled in Ryu's eyes as his fingers slid down my sides tickling my rib cage. When they found the edges of the newest scar Callahan had given me, his expression hardened.

Why?

I struggled against him, shoving at his chest to get away.

Why do you think? He's a sick bastard who gets off on my pain.

The drake king allowed me to shift off his lap, his cock leaving me hollow and empty.

No, why did you let him do this to you?

I huffed a laugh and turned my back on him. Someone like him couldn't understand. I wasn't a king. I wasn't a man. I was a princess, and a broken one at that, with a kingdom that was on the verge of destruction.

Fighting Callahan would have done nothing but bring pain and sorrow to my people and my father. I'd long decided to take what he gave me for them, even if it meant breaking me even further. It wasn't until I found out Callahan planned on killing me and taking over the kingdom the moment we were wed that I decided to fight back.

Ryu's heat brushed my back, his fingers curling over my shoulders as his lips found the side of my neck.

He did not deserve you. He will pay for what he's done... slowly. You will have him bleeding at your feet before I'm done with him.

My heart raced at his words trickling through my mind. No one had ever said something like that to me before. I'd had men plead their undying love. Declare they would go to war for me. Empty words and promises, said after sex.

Never... never had one tell me he'd torture and kill someone because of me. For me. I had set out to save my kingdom and myself, and now it seemed like I not only had allies in my corner, but someone who would burn it all just for touching me.

It was a heady feeling.

A heaviness weighed in my throat. This was all too much for me. I'd come here to save my kingdom, not get emotional about a monster. But a monster with a magical cock, a monster who still treated me better than my own fiancé.

Without a word, I moved out of Ryu's embrace and climbed out of the hot spring. I didn't care that he could see all of me as I scrambled to get dressed and away from there as fast as possible.

A part of me was sad that he let me.

Chapter 4

WHEN I WALKED into the female's quarters, I told myself I wasn't hiding from Ryu. I had to see Beautine and figure out what we were doing next for my training. We'd already started with some basic stretches, and she had shown me the different weapons. Now for some reason, I was itching to hit or cut something.

The female drakes had a whole area to themselves. The room large enough to hold several dozens, the hard dirt ground covered in an array of different animal furs and colorful material. I hadn't quite gotten the hierarchy in the seating arrangement with the raised parts of the room being occupied by different females each time I arrived. It there was one, they weren't making it clear to me.

I made my way through the females; my clumsy feet more adapt now at stepping over their tails rather than before. Something I knew we were all thankful for.

Not seeing Aryn around, I searched out Beautine in the crowd. Sitting next to her, I placed the daggers I received from training in my lap.

Beautine offered me a whetstone and mimed running it across the daggers.

Still unsure about the weapons, I fumbled around with them until Beautine's hands came on top of mine to show me the correct way to sharpen them.

Though my eyes were focused on the task at hand, I could feel the malice coming from nearby. My hands slowed and my eyes shifted toward the moving mouth next to me.

"That prissy bitch thinks she can just waltz in here and take our king?" Daylea griped with no regard for me sitting right there a few feet away, reading her lips.

Oh. Right.

"Shush," the pale blue female drake sitting beside Daylea swatted at her. "You shouldn't talk about the king's mate like that."

"She is not his mate," Daylea snarled, baring her teeth and claws at the other female.

The blue one flinched back. "She smells like it, though."

"That's because she's whoring herself out to him, nothing more." With that, Daylea shot me a nasty look.

If Aryn had been there, she would have gotten pissed on my behalf and tried to shut Daylea up, but I pretended not to understand, I wanted to see how much deeper in a hole she'd dig herself. It would also help to see if anyone else had the same or worse thoughts about me.

"You're just pissed off because King Ryu threw you aside after he caught you trying to fuck his brothers," a deep violet drake cut in as she scrunched her nose, adjusting the fabric in her lap. I didn't know how she got her stitches so small with those claws in the way.

I peered down at the daggers in my lap, trying to figure out how to best deal with this. If all the females felt this way about me, then it was going to be a problem. I needed to have their favor because that would make it easier to get the males on board.

Sure, Ryu could order them to go to battle for me. He was the drake king. But I didn't want them to fight for me because they were being forced to. No, I wanted them to believe in the cause, to fight with all their strength. That was how you won a war.

Beautine sat beside me and finally said something to Daylea. "Regardless of your opinions of her, if not for the princess, we would not know about the attack coming from Plumus. We need her kingdom as much as they need us."

Daylea's nose scrunched up as she eyeballed me. "Not if she's dead."

Okay. That was enough. Dropping the whetstone, I grabbed my daggers and faced Daylea completely.

"I am deaf, not stupid," I stated, with a snarl. "If you have something to say to me, have the courage to say it so I can understand you and not the cowardly, underhanded way. Thinking I can't read your lips? Even more insulting."

Daylea's eyes widened as her mouth dropped open, face paling at my words.

"I might be the king's whore," I gestured with smug satisfaction, "but at least I'm willing to do whatever it takes to save my people. What does that say about you?"

The other female drakes nodded around me in agreement while Daylea swallowed visibly. Climbing to her feet, she snapped at me.

"I still don't like you." Then stalked out the door.

"Oh, how will I ever go on?" I called out to her, turning back to sharpening my daggers. I was used to women like her, always trying to get the upper hand on other women in any way they could, even if it meant tearing them down.

"I'm sorry about Daylea." Beautine mouthed and rubbed her fist against her chest. I'd tried to teach her, as well as a few other drakes, how to speak in sign. Beautine had caught on far better than many of the others, even Tat. "She's just upset that you have the king's favor when he used to bed her."

"It's alright. I get it." I waved her off and focused on my task. Sharpening my daggers was one of the lessons Beautine had me working on before we got down to basics in the training ring.

"You can't learn to fight until you can learn to take care of your weapon," she had said, or something along those lines.

"There." I lifted my dagger up to get her appraisal. "When do I get to start training?"

Beautine retrieved the dagger from me and surveyed my work.

"Try a bit more force. And once you have mastered your breathing and taking care of your weapons." She offered me my daggers back, hilt first and then leaned in. "So... we've all wanted to know."

My brow arched. "Know what?"

"How does the king compare?" Beautine's eyes twinkled with mischief, and while none of the other drakes came any closer, they were all listening intently.

I licked my lips and let out a nervous laugh. "I'm not sure what you mean."

Beautine swatted at me. "Yes, you do. You've been with a drake and a human. So, which one is better?"

My head turned around the room and saw the rampant attention all the female drakes gave me. Was this what it was like to have female friends?

Back at the palace, I lost many of them after I lost my hearing and my mother. That didn't go unnoticed, which either meant my old friends didn't care to learn how to navigate my new situation or they were never my friends to begin with. Maybe both.

Heat burned my cheeks at the attention, and I focused on the daggers in my hands rather than return their intense stares.

"It was... different." I tucked a stray dark hair behind my ear. "Humans don't have the extra... uh... appendages."

I glanced up to see Beautine's reply.

"They don't have tails, you mean?"

I cleared my throat. "Or horns. Though they were useful when I needed something to grab onto."

Beautine and the other females laughed. Their delight at my words made me feel like one of them.

"Though," I began, wanting to bond with them more, "do all drake men use their tails to... uh... penetrate?"

Beautine grinned from ear to ear. "And women. There is a benefit to being a drake that makes it so that we do not need a man for pleasure if we don't want it." She shot a knowing look at her fellow drakes who nodded in agreement.

"And what of the brothers?" Beautine asked me out of the blue. "Which do you prefer?"

Her new questions made me jolt. "Wha... what do you mean? There's nothing going on with me and the king's brothers."

They couldn't possibly know about what happened with Ira in the corridor the other day. I swore we'd been alone, unless that drake blabbed to anyone who would listen. Thinking of the calculating Ira, it didn't seem his way.

"Oh, do not get embarrassed. It is normal and natural to be attracted to them too. Encouraged even." Beautine patted my hand reassuringly as one of the females who'd been with Daylea leaned forward.

"Besides, the more males you have, the more likely you will become with child."

The gleeful expression on the female's face didn't stop the choking gasp that came out of me. With child? Who? Who said anything about becoming with child?

I hadn't planned on being here long term so a child would definitely complicate things. Besides, could drakes even breed with humans?

That was a stupid question.

Of course they could. That's how they were created in the first place. Their dragon ancestors used their human forms to fuck their way through the human population until they made a whole new race of dragon human hybrids.

"Oh, that would be fantastic." Beautine took my hand in hers and beamed down at me. "Then you will certainly be one of us."

The door to the female quarters opened, and Aryn walked in with a scowl on her face. She stalked over to me and signed quickly.

"We need to talk. Alone."

Happy to have a reason to get out of this crazy discussion, I withdrew my hand from Beautine and signed back to Aryn.

"Of course, let's go."

Chapter 5
Cal

THE SCREAMS OF the soldiers hanging on Cal's dungeon wall sent a thrill of delight through him. But then he remembered... these weren't his dungeons yet. He had to find his bitch of a fiancé first.

Who knew that the deaf cunt had it in her to run to the drakes for help? It almost made Cal laugh at the absurdity of it. He had underestimated Georgia, that was for sure.

"Are you done here yet?" Luis droned from his seat nearby. "I'm hungry."

"Bored, brother?" Cal cocked a brow at the lounging prince. "You could get off your ass and help. It would make things go a lot quicker."

Lu rolled his head to the side and grimaced at the soldier's bloodied form. "You know this kind of work has never been my kind of thing."

Lu had always been more of the kind to enjoy screams of pain for pleasure rather than for business. Torturing soldiers for information didn't quite make him hard like it did Cal. There was nothing to gain from causing pain for anything other than information. Then there was the pure pleasure of getting something out of someone who swore loyalty above all else.

"Besides," Lu continued with a sigh, leaning his arm on the decrepit wooden table next to him, "didn't you get everything from this one already? We know the princess escaped to the drakes, and we know they're in the Grebe forest. What else could you possibly get from him?"

Cal shrugged. "He could have something else of use in that head of his. Gods know his comrades didn't." The prince gestured to the discarded and mutilated bodies piled up on the dirty dungeon floor.

"And what of the king?" Lu tapped his fingers on the table. "Don't you think he will notice one of his soldiers is missing?"

A wicked smile crawled up Cal's face. "Not if he thinks they were killed by the drakes. It's a good thing we intercepted them before they could reach the king, or we'd have more of a problem on our hands."

"I'm honestly surprised the princess even went to the drakes." Luis stroked his fingers up and down the surface of the table. "If she had run to anyone, I'd have imagined it would be her father first."

"One would think." Cal leaned on the wall beside the soldier, pointing his knife an inch from his eye. "What do you think? Do you think the princess should have gone to the king first?"

The soldier stayed still, his face too close to the knife to even nod.

"I'm sorry, I can't hear you. What was that?" Cal let his hand slip and cut a shallow wound across the soldier's cheek. "Oops, my hand got shaky waiting for your response."

"No," the soldier croaked out, licking his dry and cracked lips.

"See?" Cal promptly removed the knife and turned to his brother. "He doesn't think so either. Why would she run to daddy? That bitch is too proud to tell her father anything." Cal paused and tapped the tip of the knife against his chin, not bothered by the blood staining him. "No, she would want to do everything herself, leaving her pathetic king to think he had chosen a good match for her."

Luis snorted. "Hardly. Anyone with half a brain could see through your pretenses long before they let them put their hands on their precious daughter." Luis hummed and crossed one booted foot over the other. "No, the king is desperate. He knows it. We know it. I think he would have accepted just about anyone who wanted to take his daughter's hand if only to help replenish the coffers and keep them out of war."

Cal smirked at that. "That was never going to happen. If Kinoko is so easily overtaken with just an offer of marriage, others will come as well. We'll have to fight to keep it until we prove we're a force to reckon with..." Cal paused and licked his lips, the need for violence burning his veins. "After we take care of those pesky drakes."

Cal turned back to the soldier and flipped his knife over and over in his hand.

"Now, let's see if we can get something else of use out of you. Maybe I'll even spare you."

The soldier groaned and blinked one swollen eye at Cal. Hope filled the soldier's gaze, and that sent a fresh thrill through Cal.

"Spare you a boring life that is," Cal corrected himself before plunging the knife into the soldier's shoulder. His screams rang in Cal's ears, and he sighed happily. Now, if only it was higher pitched and accompanied with a pair of tits.

Then it would be perfect.

Chapter 6

ARYN LED ME away from the female quarters and back toward the king's room. My feet struggled to follow her. I didn't want to face the drake king yet, but Aryn didn't care.

"Don't be reluctant now. You've already gotten yourself planted right where you wanted," Aryn signed with a stern expression on her face. "The drakes will help, and then we can go home. So you must continue to play the part of a willing whore."

I flinched and signed back. "It's not that simple."

"Isn't it?" Aryn shifted to the side of the corridor as a set of drakes walked past us. Their golden eyes slid over to us, watching our hand movements before continuing on their way. Aryn grabbed my arm to get my attention.

"You bed the king, keep him happy, and we get our kingdom back," Aryn gestured with increasing fervor. "Callahan and his wretched brother will go to the underworld where they belong."

"And what about after?" I pulled my lower lip between my teeth and chewed on it. "The drakes..." I paused, not sure how to continue. "They're going to want to remain allies."

"So?" Aryn's brows furrowed, her shoulders shifting. "We could use them against any oncoming attacks."

She didn't get it.

Aryn thought it was as simple as having sex with the king until Cal was gone. It wasn't simple. It was far from it.

Ryu's possessive hold on me, his marking on my inner thigh, and now his brother's interest in me. It made my stomach twist into knots. It knew they weren't going to just let me go back to my life in the palace. Nor would I want them to be forced to hide out here in the mountains anymore after they helped us. Kinoko would owe them a debt too great to repay with simply my body.

"But at what costs?" I sighed and walked away from her.

With no particular destination in mind, I stalked down the hallway. Thankfully, Aryn didn't follow. I needed a moment alone. A moment to think about the situation I'd gotten myself into.

When I first had this idea, I thought it was the answer to all my problems. Now... I might have made things worse.

Saving the kingdom was one thing. Finding my way out of the entanglement with the king and his brothers... that was another.

My mind wandered back to what Ira said to me.

You're broken just like I am. They don't understand. They could never understand.

Broken? Ha. I'd show him broken. Ira might think the loss of his eye meant he was broken, but I sure as hell didn't. And I definitely didn't want him to treat me like a broken toy.

Before I knew it, my feet led me to the edge of the market. Drakes wandered around from booth to booth without a care in the world. The ground and very air vibrated with the amount of hustle and bustle coming from the area.

I didn't know how many of them knew about the imminent danger sitting on their doorstep. Since Beautine knew, I could only assume everyone did. Unless Ryu only told a select few? Either way, I envied their bliss.

I stepped further into the marketplace, and several drakes nearby at a booth stopped what they were doing to stare at me.

Hesitant to cause another scene, like the last time I was there, I peered down at the fabrics at their stalls. The cloth was the most beautiful I'd ever seen. A longing burned in my chest, but I forced myself to step back, turning to go.

A female drake of cobalt scales who was working the stall waved her hand at me to stop. Her mouth moved, and as the other drakes started to move on, I could only guess what she told them. As they moved, she gestured me forward.

Part of me didn't want to offend her. But her gesture encouraged the part of me drawn to the glimmering fabrics. Chewing on my lower lip, I inched forward, my eyes flicking to the different shades on the counter. Emerald greens, blacks so dark that it sucked the light in around it, and a sparkling bronze.

The drake placed her hand on the bronze one and arched a brow. Her lips moved, this time where I could see them.

"You like?"

Licking my lips, I nodded and smoothed my hand over the material. It caressed my fingers in a way I'd never felt before, and I couldn't wait to feel it against my skin.

The female lifted the fabric and held it out to me with an eager smile.

I glanced at it and then back to her, shaking my head then gesturing to myself. I had nothing to pay for it. All my money was back at the palace and besides, I didn't think the drakes took gold coins in payment. A quick glance at the other booths showed none of them were using coins to pay.

A hand on mine drew my attention back to the drake before me. She tapped the metal bracelet on my wrist. It was something one of the other drakes had given me to wear.

I frowned at her and then back at the bracelet. She tapped it again and then the fabric, flicking her finger between us as her lips formed one word.

"Trade."

Blinking at her, I realized she wanted me to trade the bracelet for the fabric.

Nodding eagerly, I unclipped the bracelet and handed it over to her. Grinning brightly, the female drake handed me the fabric, her eyes focusing on the bracelet's sparkling gems.

You should have asked for more.

I spun around, searching for the growling voice in my head only to find the drake king's other brother, Desmond, standing behind me, carving an apple with a sharp claw. He popped a slice into his mouth and jerked his chin at the female drake. She frowned at the prince, brows furrowed in irritation.

What do you mean? I thought at him.

The prince stepped to the booth, and his lips moved too fast for me to keep up as he talked to the female drake. Her face scrunched up at the prince's words, glancing from the fabric to the bracelet and back. Whatever the prince was saying made her unhappy. Then she inclined her head once and held up another bit of fabric to me of an emerald, green color.

Desmond's head twisted to me, and he tilted his chin toward it.

Take it.

Face scrunching in confusion, I took the fabric offered to me and thanked the female drake. Turning to Desmond, I cocked my head to the side.

What was that about?

You should be more careful out here on your own. The female was trying to cheat you. Your bracelet is far more valuable than the fabric she was offering. I simply made her give you what it was worth.

I frowned down at the fabric and then back at the female, who had turned to another customer. Then I lifted my head to Desmond and favored him with a small smile.

"Thank you."

Desmond shook his head, the auburn color of his hair a deeper shade than his brothers'. Still, they could almost be twins if not for the way Desmond's lips twisted up into a mischievous grin, flashing a set of fangs at me.

Don't mention it. Let me walk with you.

I hesitated to accept. I'd had few interactions with the brother and none of them were pleasant. Why was he being nice to me now? However, I wanted to know what was in the drake's mind and the only way to do it was to let him accompany me.

Come now, princess, Desmond teased my mind. *I won't bite unless you ask me to.*

That's what I was afraid of.

Chapter 7

DESMOND WALKED ALONG beside me as I skimmed over each stall in the market. Every once in a while, he'd point something out and explain it in my mind before I could ask. It was both helpful and extremely irritating.

Then there was the way the other drakes reacted with him around. Each time I stopped to look at something, the drake behind the stall brightened, but then took one look at Desmond and became a little less enthused.

I paused in front of a food vendor with what smelled of honey glazed duck, my mouth watering with hunger. The drake behind the stall saw me looking, my tongue tucked between my cheek and my teeth. Before I could tell him I didn't have anything to trade, the shimmery chestnut colored drake shoved a cloth wrapped duck in my hands.

Shaking my head, I held it back out to him unsure how to explain my lack of funds.

Desmond's claw curled around my shoulder, his voice whispering in my mind.

Take it.

Scowling at him, I made myself speak out loud so as not to be rude to the drake watching us with interest.

"Just like that? You say I can have it so I should? I will not steal from him. I have nothing to pay him for it."

Desmond's lips ticked up at my snarled words. That wasn't the reaction I wanted. Instead of answering me, he pointed at the owner of the stall.

The drake smiled politely and moved his lips slowly. "It's a gift."

My lips pursed.

See? Desmond's voice smugly filtered through my head. *Do not insult him by refusing.*

Still not convinced that I should, I clasped the duck closer and inclined my head in thanks. I waited until we walked away from the stall before stalking at a quickened pace away from the drake prince.

I ducked into a side tunnel, not sure which way I was really going. I just wanted to get away from Desmond before I throttled him. I came to a fork in the tunnel and struggled to read the markings on the wall.

Was it left to go back to the women's quarters or right?

I felt the heat of his body before I saw him over my shoulder. Desmond stood close behind me, a curious yet playful look in his eyes. When I gave him my attention, he cocked his head to the side almost like the dog the cook had in the kitchen whenever he wanted to be petted.

Go away. I shoved the thought at him with enough force there was no way he didn't receive it.

Desmond's smile widened until the tips of his fangs peaked out. *And leave you to get lost in the tunnels? Ryu would punish me severely for such carelessness.*

My eyes narrowed into slits. *I'm not your concern and if you'd left well enough alone, I wouldn't feel like I just stole something for the first time in my life.*

One brow curled up and then Desmond's head tipped back, his mouth opening wide as his chest shook with his laugh. A snarl built up into my chest, and before I knew it, I threw the duck at the drake prince's head.

Desmond pulled back as the duck bounced off his face, more surprised than hurt by my attack. Blinking at me, Desmond glanced down at the duck on the ground.

Did you just... throw that duck at me?

Yes, I snapped, closing the distance between us. I shoved a finger at his chest, wincing at the hard muscle beneath it. *You can't just bully anyone you want into giving you free things. People have the right to make a living. Even drakes.*

Desmond snatched the finger pointing at his chest. I gasped and pulled my feet moving but the rest of me not following. Desmond jerked me forward until my front pressed against his firm chest, the spines of his armor poking me.

You of all people shouldn't assume you know what is going on. His lips moved while his words tickled my mind, his breath hot on my face.

I know you and your brothers use your status to do whatever you want. Your people are afraid of you. I can see it whenever you're around, I shot back, glaring into his face.

Desmond's lips twisted to the side in a smirk. He used one claw to brush my hair away from my face.

The fear you see is laced with respect. You can rule with fear as well as love and still be respected. Drakes are not like humans. The strongest survive. Any weakness will be exploited. We cannot afford to let ourselves be loved by the drakes when they are always plotting to take our places.

My lips turned down in confusion. *That sounds like a lonely way to live.*

Shrugging a shoulder, Desmond released me but didn't step back. *We may have human ancestors, but do not mistake us for having human morals.*

I shook my head. *That still doesn't give you the right to just steal from your people.*

Desmond rolled his eyes and tipped my chin up with a clawed finger.

If you'd been patient and not stomped away, you'd have seen I paid the drake myself.

I started to retort and then frowned, pressing my lips firmly together.

Oh.

Yes. Oh. He stroked along the line of my jaw, his fingers leaving a hot trail in its wake.

I shuddered, the desire to pull back almost as big as the one to let him touch me further. What was with the drake royalty? I let one of them defile me and now my traitorous body wanted the rest of them to join in.

The thought of Ryu was enough to make me lick my dry lips and step back from Desmond. I inclined my head and signed thank you before darting away and down the hall. I didn't even think about the fact he didn't know what I'd signed until I was standing back in front of the female's quarters.

Chapter 8
Ira

IRA'S ONE GOOD eye watched the human princess run down the tunnels, leaving his brother standing alone with a dumbfounded expression on his face. Ira stepped out of the shadows of the adjacent tunnel, a brow arched in his brother's direction.

"Do I even want to ask what that was about?"

Desmond's gaze flicked over to his brother before he bent at the waist and picked up the discarded duck. He unwrapped it from its cloth and took a large bite of it.

Ira grimaced, saying nothing of his brother's disgusting habits.

"We just had a disagreement." Desmond chewed the duck in contemplation before adding, "She doesn't think much of us, does she?"

Shrugging one shoulder, Ira leaned against the tunnel wall. "We haven't given her much reason to think we are anything other than vicious brutes. After all, that is what the rest of the world sees. Why should she be any different?"

Desmond snorted. "If you'd stop playing with her, then maybe she'd see us differently."

"What's the fun in that?" Ira's lips curved up in a vicious smile. "Besides, I'm hardly the one playing with her. Ryu is far more enamored with her than I am. I swear, if he growls at me one more time for even looking her way, I'm going to roast him."

Shaking his head with a laugh, Desmond used the cloth of the duck to wipe his mouth. "Like that'd do anything other than piss him off."

They set out down the corridor, easily navigating the tunnels to where they needed to be. Living underground had its disadvantages. No sunlight, plus the air became stale after a while. Ryu had done much to give new life to the mountain, including having the brightest minds of the drakes build an air filtration system. No one, not even dragons, wanted to smell dirt and decay all the time.

Passing by the entrance to the royal hot springs, Ira grunted. "By the way, if he hasn't ordered it already, we need the water cleaned. Ryu fucked her in there again."

Desmond grimaced. "Why can't he defile the princess somewhere that isn't being used by all of us?"

"Because he's the king?" Ira arched his brow with a knowing look. "And you better watch yourself. The old ones help us if one of us touch his precious princess."

Huffing a laugh, Desmond smacked his brother on the shoulder.

"I've never seen that stop you before. If I remember correctly, you specifically went out of your way to seduce Wellern when you knew that Ryu thought abour adding her to his rotation."

"He's already got a big head. It's good for him to struggle for what he wants once in a while." Ira paused and smiled in memory. "Besides, Wellern wouldn't have been happy with Ryu's way of rutting. She liked it when I wrapped my hands around her —"

"Okay, okay. Stop." Desmond waved his hands in front of him. "I don't need details. I don't want to know what Wellern likes. And I suggest you keep those words to yourself before we get to Ryu, or he'll really bite your head off."

Ira's good eye crinkled at the edges. "And I suppose I shouldn't mention how you were flirting with the princess in the corridors just now."

Desmond paused, his mouth dropping open slightly. "That wasn't flirting. That was keeping the market from taking advantage of her."

"And I see she appreciated your efforts so much," Ira mused as he paused before their private dining area.

Rubbing the back of his neck, Desmond grimaced. "It's harder than I thought to communicate with her just through her mind. Some things don't come through right, and then there's the whole 'everyone else can't hear what you're saying to each other' thing. It would be so much easier just to talk to her."

Ira grabbed a goblet off the table and filled it with the dark liquid from the jug beside it.

"Perhaps you should learn her language instead. Make things easier for her."

Desmond filled a plate randomly. Ira wasn't even sure he was paying attention to what he was putting on it. He almost reminded Desmond that he didn't like onions when he put them on his plate, but then thought better of it. It'd be far more entertaining to see if he actually ate it to save face or not.

"How am I supposed to learn her language? I can't come out and ask her to teach it to me." Desmond made a face and flopped down onto the stone seat by the fire pit.

Ira watched him with growing amusement as Desmond picked up a long stalk of onion and brought it to his mouth, his mind so engrossed with his thoughts he didn't notice the vegetable until he'd bit into it.

"Ugh. Fuck. Gross. Why did I get onions?"

Throwing his head back and laughing, Ira took up his seat across from him, his own plate balancing on his knee.

"Finally noticed, did you?"

Desmond shot Ira a glare before throwing the stalk of onion at him.

"You're such a bastard."

Ira shrugged his shoulder.

"So, are you going to help me or just watch me poison myself?"

"Ate another onion, brother?"

Ira and Desmond's heads turned to where Ryu walked in the room, a broad grin on his face. Ira had to admit his brother might be more possessive and growly about his new toy, but he seemed far happier now that he was getting his dick wet regularly.

"Fuck you too." Desmond growled, slouching over his plate and staring hard at its contents.

"We were just discussing how to learn the princess's hand language," Ira provided, watching his older brother's movements closely for a reaction.

Ryu paused by the serving table and frowned. "I do not know the language she and her maid use. How would we learn it?"

"I caught her teaching her guard, Tatoween, before. Perhaps we should ask him?" Ira asked, flicking a bit of onion that'd landed on him off his leg.

Desmond shook his head as he dragged his fingers up his left horn. "Why learn second hand and not go straight to the source?"

Ryu and Ira exchanged a look before breaking out into a growling laugh. Smacking Desmond on the back of the head as he passed by, Ryu sat in the remaining spot around the fire.

"You have met the princess, yes? Do you really think she will give up her secret language to us?"

"To make her and our lives easier? If we could learn the language, then we could teach it to the other drakes. Then I know I would feel much better with her wandering the corridors alone," Desmond explained, not realizing his words caused Ryu's jaw to clench and his chest to burn with rage.

"She did what?" Ryu snarled, his plate completely forgotten as he focused on Desmond. "When was she out by herself? Why wasn't her guard with her? I'm going to —"

Ira stopped his brother with a hand on his arm. "Take a moment. You cannot confront her in a rage, or she will just continue to defy you. Control yourself."

Ryu almost snapped at Ira then seemed to think better of it. With much effort, Ryu blew out a breath, the air flickering with flames before him.

"Fine. What do you suggest?"

Playing with the meat on his plate, Ira smiled secretly. "If you cannot go to the source, go to the one who cares about her even more than you do."

"I don't care for her," Ryu protested.

Ira ignored him and continued. "The princess may not care for her wellbeing, but her maid surely does. If we implore her to help us, then I'm sure that we can find a mutually beneficial solution to our problem."

"And you think she'll help us?" Desmond cocked his head to the side, adjusting the armor on his shoulder. "She doesn't exactly trust us."

"For the sake of her princess, she will."

Both of his brothers stared at him for a long minute.

"Very well," Ryu announced at last. "Since it was your idea, you can persuade the maid to assist us."

Ira didn't so much as protest. He was used to his brothers pushing the difficult tasks in his direction. Most of the time, they didn't even realize he had orchestrated it to be that way.

If Ira became endeared to the handmaiden, then he would the trust of someone who knew the inner workings of the princess's mind. That, in itself, was far more valuable than any hardship he would face convincing the older human female to help them learn their secret language.

"Very well." Ira sat his plate and goblet to the side and stood. "I suppose the task goes to the smartest and cleverest of us. I will try not to fail you, brothers."

They threw bits of meat and vegetables at his back as he made his way out of the dining room. They could be so ungrateful.

Chapter 9

SWEAT POURED DOWN my brow and tickled the small of my back. I hadn't perspired so much since I learned to sneak out of the castle when I was thirteen. The way Beautine looked at me, I had a feeling this wouldn't be the last time.

Three days of being stuck in this training room with its high domed ceiling and hard walls lined with every kind of weapon imaginable, and I didn't feel as if I was getting much better. My body hurt in all the wrong ways. Muscles I'd never used before screamed at me in protest.

"Hands up," Beautine commanded me, her lips moving slow enough for me to keep up while she showed what she wanted me to do. "Don't let me through your defenses."

I pursed my lips, concentrating on my stance, my movements, even the way I breathed. Beautine told me everything counted when you were fighting. Since I didn't have one of my senses to rely on I had to make up for it with all the others.

"Feel the air move around you." She thrust a fist toward me, letting me feel the air shift with her movement.

Automatically, my body moved to avoid the fist coming at me.

Beautine grinned and nodded. "Again."

We went through several movements, my eyes searching for the signs of where she would move and when. I never knew my way of reading people would have a use such as combat. If I'd known maybe I would have... against Cal... fuck. No. Don't think about him now.

Stuck in my memories, I didn't notice the slight shift of balance as Beautine whipped around, her tail hit the back of my knees. I landed on my front hard, the breath knocked out of me.

Grunting, I pushed myself up to my hands and knees.

Beautine stood over me. Her hand held out to me, she waited until I grasped it and stood.

"Never get distracted," she instructed. "That's when you end up dead."

I grunted and nodded my understanding. It was a bit like dancing. Figuring out where your partner would move next by the shift of their body weight. Even if I never saw battle, the ability to protect myself against anyone, not even Cal and Luis, lifted a huge weight off my chest.

Beautine arched her brows and waved a hand. "Again?"

Before I could answer, Beautine's head whipped to the side. My eyes followed her movements to settle on Ryu standing in the entrance to the training room. He walked toward us with confidence in each step, his tail barely moving behind him as if he had complete control over every aspect of his body.

I licked my lips and stepped back. My body quivered with the mere presence of the drake king standing there, staring at me like I was the next thing he wanted to take a bite out of.

My single step back caused Ryu's lips to curl up with a vicious, knowing smirk, his fangs peeking out from between his lips. Just seeing those fangs made the mark on my inner thigh pulsate and ache for him. I didn't know how this creature caused such a visceral reaction from me with just one look. Worse, the way his nostrils flared told me that he knew exactly how I reacted to him.

I think you need a new teacher.

Beautine glanced from me and then back to Ryu before bowing her head slightly and leaving without a word.

Traitor.

Ryu took up the space where Beautine had stood a moment ago, his hand reaching behind him to pull the halberd from his back. My lips curled as I thought at him.

Do you carry that thing everywhere with you?

If I didn't, then you'd have stabbed me already, I'm sure.

I huffed a laugh. *I can't stab you if I need you to fight my betrothed for me. So stabbing you would be counterintuitive.*

Do you really want me to be the one to kill your betrothed? Wouldn't you rather do it yourself?

The thought had occurred to me, especially when Beautine had offered to help me learn to fight for myself. The idea of having Cal and Luis at the tip of my blade, at my mercy, was almost too much for me. The very thought sent a shiver of delight down my spine, and to my utter horror, heat spouted between my legs.

I see you like that idea. Ryu stepped toward me holding his weapon before him. *Let me show you how.*

A part of me thought this was a bad idea. The other part was eager to see the drake king on his back at my mercy, like he'd had me many times over the course of the last few days. The more times the drake king touched me, fucked me, and completely and absolutely owned my body, the more I wanted him and felt like I was no longer the seducer but the one getting seduced.

Still, I was hesitant because of the strength in his arms and viciousness in his face. I pushed that aside and held up the daggers Beautine had been teaching me with.

Alright. What do you want me to do?

Ryu lifted a hand and bent his fingers in a come-hither movement.

I frowned, unsure what he wanted me to do. I wasn't just going to come at him. That would be suicide and a sure way to get me on my back once more.

Come, little one. Attack me. He flexed his claws and smirked. *Or are you scared?*

Baiting me. That's all this was. He wanted me to get mad and charge at him head on. What he didn't know was I was used to people trying to get me upset because of my disability. Or speak about me when I was in the room, thinking I couldn't understand them. I had to school my emotions and face to keep from causing a political incident.

So, instead of rushing him, I took my time inching around the training area, searching for a weak point on the large drake king. My gaze skimmed over his muscular form, lingering on the spikes coming out of his metal and bone shoulder guards and greaves. I wanted to stay away from those for sure. My eyes flicked to his long tongue sliding along the edges of his lips and tonguing his fangs.

Heat pooled between my thighs. Ryu sniffed the air and smirked my way, the extra swish in his tail giving away his glee.

Shit. This was going to be harder than I thought.

I waited too long to act. Ryu shot toward me, almost a blur of movement from his speed. Sucking in a gasp of air, I barely stepped back before Ryu had his tail wrapped around my ankle, jerking me off my feet. Bracing myself for the ground to hit my back the way it did with Beautine, Ryu shocked me by catching me around the waist.

Come now, your enemies will not wait for you to come to them. One clawed hand cupped me beneath the chin, holding my face up to him. *You will be a mighty warrior and all those who see you will tremble before you.*

My lips curled up into a smile. *You don't need to lie to make me feel better. I know I am hardly intimidating.*

Ryu brought me back up to my full height, moving in close to me. His finger slid the shoulder of my shirt to the side, exposing one of the many scars covering my body. The claw of his finger tickled along its puffed-up edges.

There is more to a warrior than a fierce and horrifying exterior. That finger moved down into the neck of my shirt, tracing around the line of my breast and pressing his hand over my heart. *Your heart is filled with such fire, it would frighten even the bravest of warriors.*

I scoffed, turning my head to the side. *I couldn't even stand up to Callahan and Luis.* My eyes burned with tears of frustration. *I had to run to someone bigger and stronger to help me fight.*

Ryu turned my face back to him and leaned forward. His tongue laved at my face, picking up the tears that had escaped.

Even the strongest of warriors know when it's time to fight and when it's time to wait for reinforcements. It doesn't make you weak. It makes you strong.

Licking my lips, I swallowed thickly, this time letting my voice come out.

"Okay. Show me what to do."

Right. Ryu stepped back and pushed us back up, giving me a teasing smile as he got back into position. *Let's see if the little one has teeth after all.*

Chapter 10
Desmond

THE YOUNGER PRINCE of the drakes had no problem seducing females to get what he wanted. It was one of his favorite pastimes to be sure. Usually what he wanted was a quick and dirty rut against the mountain's walls, but today was different.

The human handmaiden, Aryn, could not be seduced. Oh, he could definitely get her on her back, screaming for more, but that wasn't the goal here. Besides, Desmond didn't think the princess would be too happy if he fucked her handmaiden. Especially if he ever planned to be at the mercy of her delicious form.

No.

Desmond had to find a way to get to Aryn's good side so she would help his brothers and him learn the language she did with the princess. They couldn't have them talking, conspiring against the drakes right under their very noses. Plus, it would certainly get him into the good graces of a certain fiery princess.

Finding the princess, now that was easy. Desmond could find her with his eyes shut and his ears covered. All he had to do was follow the mouthwatering scent of cinnamon, juicy raspberries, and something sharp that cut his nose. Of course, even her scent would be lethal. It fit with her personality so well.

Desmond sauntered toward the female's quarters. It was the obvious place to look for the little human maid. She didn't have the backbone and bravery the princess had. It would surprise him if Aryn walked any of these corridors alone. The guard she had assigned to her complained enough about having to ride her ass all day. If Desmond knew Vion, the asshole would have dropped her at the female's quarters when she became too much of a nuisance.

Stopping before the double doors, Desmond inclined his head at the two guards standing watch. Cadben and Baron were two sides of the same coin. One could be your best friend in moments, and the other was more likely to stab you first, ask your name later.

"Your Highness," Baron grunted, his voice low and gravelly. He stepped to the side with no other words exchanged.

Cadben did no such thing. The blue drake beamed at him, striking up a conversation.

"Prince Desmond, did you see that fight in the west corridor? I thought for sure B'ven would take Kir down, but the sly snake ended up pulling through at the end."

Desmond shook his head and clapped a hand on the drake's shoulder. "Unfortunately, I missed it. You'll have to tell me about it some other time."

"Yes, of course." Cadben nodded eagerly. "I look forward to it."

Baron snorted. "He's just being polite. He doesn't want to hear about a stupid fight. His Highness has more pressing matters that don't involve our pathetic squabbles."

Frowning, Cadben avoided Desmond's face and stepped aside.

"Sorry, Your Highness. Didn't mean to keep you from your work."

"Baron is right," Desmond admitted with a sigh. "I can't focus on the fight right now, but I wasn't lying about wanting to hear about it. Perhaps later?"

Cadben's head jerked up and his eyes lit up. "Yes, Your Highness. Of course."

Happy that he had saved the drake's feelings, Desmond pushed into the female's quarters with a lopsided fang toothed grin.

"My lovely creatures of grace and beauty, it has been too long."

The females paused what they were doing at his appearance. A few of them turned back to their tasks while the younger females, the ones ripe for mating, swarmed him with eager glee.

"Your Highness, have you seen my new necklace? I made it myself."

"Look at this dagger. Isn't the inlay gorgeous?"

"Why haven't you called on me? I thought we had fun."

Desmond held his palms up and shook his head with a laugh. "My lovelies, I would love to say this is a social visit, but I do have a reason for coming here that doesn't involve pleasure." He said the word so it ended in a growl, sending the arousal of the females spiking in the room.

"What do you need? Anything, my prince," one of the closer drake females, purred. Ordya, he thought her name was, leaned closer, her pale-yellow scales gleaming in the light. "Anything at all."

Pushing down his own mating urges, Desmond scanned the room for the one he had come for. Not seeing the small woman, he turned back to the females at his feet.

"Where is the human female? The shorter, plumper one, Aryn? I have need of her."

A round of disappointed sounds filled his ears, leaving him wishing he could calm their fears, but he was on a mission.

"Ugh," Daylea snarled from his left side. "What is so special about these human females? Do they have ale flavored nipples? Do their cunts dance upon your cocks?"

A few of the females giggled at Daylea's words. Others shot Daylea glares and disapproving looks. The females were still split in their opinion of Georgia and Aryn. Desmond had hoped they would have come along further than that by now.

Pursing his lips, Desmond turned to Daylea. He grasped her chin between his clawed fingers, causing her eyes to widen and her pulse to race in his ears.

"I could never find a human more appealing than one of my kind..." He let his claws tighten, biting into her scaled flesh. "If you disrespect our visitors in my presence again, I will make sure that they are the last words you will ever speak, am I clear?"

Daylea swallowed and tried to nod but couldn't against Desmond's grip.

Desmond released her with enough force to send her stumbling back. Sensing his anger, the females back away from him, a mixture of fear coating the arousal in the air.

"Now," he turned to the other females, "who can assist me in finding the human, Aryn?"

"I can." A smaller female of a bright sapphire blue stepped forward. She shrank back against the glares given by some of the other females but kept coming.

"Wonderful, thank you for your help..." Desmond wrapped an arm around her shoulders, giving her an encouraging squeeze. "I don't believe I know your name."

"Mai, prince... Highness... I mean, Your Highness." She stuttered over her words, tugging on the long dark blue strands of her hair braided down the side of her face and over her shoulder. "My name is Mai."

"Well, then Mai. Where can I find my prey?" I let the teasing tone in my voice smooth over the tension in the room.

Swallowing first, Mai wrung her hands together, her claws bitten to the quicks. "Aryn likes to work in the kitchens. You'll probably find her there."

"Getting in the cook's way, no doubt," another female he couldn't identify snorted causing a good-natured laugh. Desmond let that one go, or he'd be here all day.

"Very well. It seems as if my search continues." Desmond released Mai and headed for the door. "As always, my lovelies, it has been a pleasure."

Desmond ducked out of the room before any of them could attach themselves to his person. He didn't interact with the guards this time, not wanting to be distracted from his mission.

The kitchens were in a different part of the mountain, near the north entrance so they could access the river that ran nearby. The closer Desmond came to the kitchens, the more the air filled with the savory scent of meat and sweetness of the rolls being made for the evening meal. Desmond's stomach growled its approval as he stepped into the warm room.

Unlike the females' quarters, the kitchens held a half dozen drakes, maybe more. Many of them rushed back and forth to this task or that. Meanwhile, Bry, the head cook, bit the heads off anyone messing something up or distracting their colleagues.

Personally, Desmond tried to stay away from the kitchens. Bry didn't particularly like him.

"Ah, Your Highness." Bry greeted him on sight. "Come to destroy half my kitchen again? If so, let me know now so that I can give up on tonight's meal."

Desmond grimaced.

At the tender age of thirteen, Desmond thought he could light the stoves in the kitchen without so much as any accelerants. Turns out, he could. Desmond just didn't know how to turn off his fire breathing on his own. It wasn't until someone dumped a bucket of cold water on him did the fire stop pouring out of his mouth. His throat had burned for a week afterward.

"No, Bry, I'm actually here for the human, Aryn. I was told she spends her time here?" Desmond's gaze searched the room, his lips turned down in a frown at the lack of the small plump woman's figure.

"Ah, yes. *Her*." Bry rolled his eyes. Seemed she'd made an enemy of the cook as well. "I sent her to get water with one of the others. She should still be there."

"Wonderful." Desmond clasped his hands together and hurried across the kitchen. Lingering seemed like it would be bad for his health and his stomach. Ignoring the protest of said organ, Desmond walked down the corridors to the entrance of the underwater cavern.

The river ran under the mountain on this side before exiting on the other. The openings of the mountain were too small and narrow for anyone to infiltrate, making it one of the safer areas so close to the outside world.

Mahani stood at the entrance, watching his charge fill one bucket after another. He glanced my way once before turning back to his duty with a bored expression on his face. Desmond had always liked Mahani, he didn't put on airs. None of this 'yes, Your Highness, no Your Highness.' He did his job, and that was that. You either gained his trust and respect or you were dirt beneath his boot.

The drake with Aryn noticed me first. He was a young male, his horns barely coming in on his citrine head. The little knobs poked up between the tuffs of silvery white hair thrown haphazardly into a braid. He stood at attention, dropping his bucket full of water as a result.

"By the gods, you are useless, Quil'n." Aryn scowled down at her soaked skirt. She still hadn't noticed Desmond standing nearby. "It's no wonder Bry sent you to get water. I'm starting to wonder if your egg was dropped before you were born."

"Actually," Desmond interrupted. "We are born like mammals, not dragons. A bit confusing, I'm sure, for those who do not know us personally."

Aryn's gaze jerked around to Desmond, her eyes going wide. The bucket in her hand hung there just seconds from she spilled its contents.

"Uh... Your Highness. We were just..."

"It's fine." Desmond stopped her from rambling on. "I was just looking for you."

"Whatever for?" The older female's brows furrowed, her eyes filling with suspicion. This might be harder than Desmond thought.

"I need a favor."

Chapter 11
Cal

FLESH SLAPPING AGAINST flesh filled the air. The stink of sweat and sex clogged his nose in the best of ways.

"Oh, fuck, gods, just like that, Your Highness. Fuck me," the bitch screamed beneath Cal. Whether her cries of pleasure were real or faked, Cal didn't particularly care. She was nothing more than a hole for him to find his release.

Cal thrusted a few more times into the whore before pulling out and releasing his load all over her back and hair with a satisfied grunt. Pulling out of her, he threw a cloth at her.

"Get out."

The dark-haired woman with large tits didn't linger or ask questions. She quickly swiped what she could of his cum off her and gathered her clothes. Half dressed, she hurried through the bedroom door just as Luis opened it.

"I see your tastes have changed," Luis commented with a hint of humor in his tone. "Tired of petite little blondes?"

Cal ignored his brother's taunts and went to the wash bin. Using a rag, he cleansed himself of the bitch's cunt and scent. It horrified him that he had to pay for his sexual release now. Cal was attractive. He could have any woman in court or employed at the palace under him with just a cruck of his finger.

Unfortunately, none of those women were Georgia.

"What news do you have for me?" Cal asked, jerking his pants back into place and walking to the nearby table for a drink.

"I thought it was peculiar that you requested someone with such dark hair and voluptuous figure," Lu continued as if he hadn't heard him. "Then I thought maybe you grew bored with fucking the same hole every time. Now, I realized it's because she looks like your betrothed." Lu's lips curled up at the side. "Feeling a bit frustrated, brother?"

Not even bothering to set down his glass of wine, Call pulled a dagger from his waist and threw it at his brother's head.

Naturally, Luis dodged it with a smirk. "Touchy subject. I see."

"I won't miss next time," Cal threatened and then drained his glass before refilling it. "Now, tell me what I want to know. And it better be something good, or I'll have to bring that bitch back and slit her throat. I really don't want to find another whore to take her place."

Luis cocked a brow. "Testy today it seems." When Cal shot him a warning look, Luis conceded. "Very well. We haven't found a way into the mountain… yet. But our soldiers are scouring every inch until we find a way in. If there is one, they'll find it."

"Of course, there's a way in, otherwise how would those monsters be hiding there? They didn't just dig under it, there had to be a way in," Cal muttered more to himself than to his brother.

"Don't worry, brother. We'll find it." Luis stepped forward and patted Cal on the back. "Then we'll find the princess and this kingdom will be ours."

"If that old coot doesn't ruin it for us first," Cal snarled, flopping down into the chair at the table. "One word from him and the whole thing could go up in smoke."

"That brings me to the next piece of news." Luis clicked his tongue and frowned. "The king's noticed his soldiers are missing."

Cal snorted. "That was bound to happen eventually," he stated, not bothered by his brother's admission. The fact that the

Kinoko king hadn't noticed until now said something about the ruler, and none of it was good. Cal would never let his soldiers not report in immediately, and the lax security around the palace made it even worse.

"That is not the concerning part," Luis continued, a pinch between his brows. "Those guards we didn't think were watching saw when we disposed of the bodies and ratted us out to the king." He paused, watching Cal for his reaction.

Cal blinked at his brother. "And?"

"And the king has called us to come to him and explain ourselves." Luis picked at his nails, before flicking a piece of lint off his shirt. He paused for a long moment, letting Cal take in his words. "How do you want to proceed?"

That old king was getting on Cal's last nerve. He was lucky that Cal had any interest in his third-rate kingdom. If it weren't for Cal, the other kingdoms would have swooped in and taken over. Then they'd have decimated the countryside and people before killing the king and probably his pain in the ass daughter. King Fergus should be kissing Cal's ass and not questioning his every move.

"Cal?"

Jaw clenched and hands curled at his side, Cal contemplated his choices. On the one hand, he could come clean and make up some kind of story to explain why he'd tortured and killed his soldiers. None of them could tell anyone where the princess was located before they died, and while that put Cal on the winning side, it could pose a problem in the long run if he didn't pass along that information to the king.

"Cal? What are we going to do?" Luis's incessant questioning pushed Cal's nerves.

"I don't know," Cal muttered as he dragged his shirt on and buttoned it up with quick fingers.

When he finished, he looked down and found the buttons misaligned.

With a scream of frustration, Cal ripped the shirt open, buttons flying across the room. He jerked the shirt off and threw it on the ground, stomping on it with his boot until it was a crumpled mess on the floor. Chest heaving, Cal glared down at the shirt before shooting his gaze up to Luis.

"Let's get this over with."

"What are we going to tell the king?" Luis asked again, handing him a clean shirt.

"Fucking whatever we want."

"And if he doesn't accept that answer and wants more?" Luis prodded, arching a brow amusement on his face at Cal's actions.

"We kill him and make it look like an accident, then take the kingdom as our own and destroy anyone who gets in our way." Cal stalked out the door.

"Even my cunt of a betrothed."

Chapter 12

"AGAIN," BEAUTINE SIGNED for the hundredth time in the last hour.

My arm burned, seconds away from falling off. Beautine said my arm strength was lacking, and if I wanted to slice Cal's head off, I'd have to get a lot stronger. Hence the relentless swinging.

"Switch," Beautine gestured with her hands.

With an exhausted sigh, I moved the sword to my other hand. I wouldn't complain. I needed to do this. I had to do this.

Just imagine Cal's smug face as my sword sliced through his neck. Of course, I wouldn't make it that easy for him. First, I'd tie him down so he couldn't get away. If I cared about anyone hearing him, I'd shove a dirty rag in his mouth like Luis used to hold his hand over mine, the stinking sweat of his palm burning into my face.

Then I'd carve into him bit by bit. Each slice would be deeper than the last until I covered his body in cuts. We'd be twins in that respect. Maybe I would cut my name into his flesh, right across the dick he pressed against me every time he cut into me. He might not have raped me, but he had violated me in a whole other way.

My eyes burned, and my chest grew tight. I couldn't even see the training room or Beautine anymore. All I saw was Cal and Luis's grinning faces. Enjoying every minute of my pain, every tear that streaked down my face, just like the blood that had stained so many of my clothes. It had taken Aryn forever to clean them in secret.

A hand grabbed my shoulder, and I screamed, swinging around

my sword. Beautine caught it before it cut her head off, blood dripping off her hand and onto the dirt floor. I dropped the sword with a horrified gasp, rushing to Beautine's side.

"I'm sorry. I'm sorry," I signed as well as spoke out loud. I grabbed her wrist, trying to see the extent of her injury.

Beautine shrugged and pulled her hand away to sign to me. "I'm fine. You aren't the first to injure me."

My lips pressed together in a tight frown. "But I shouldn't have gotten so distracted."

Placing her good hand on my shoulder, Beautine smiled, her lips moving slowly.

"I am proud of you. Your strength of body now matches the strength in your heart."

My eyes burned for a whole different reason now. I threw myself at the female drake, wrapping my arms around her middle and burying my face in her neck. Beautine's chest rumbled with laughter beneath my face, while she patted me on the back. Rubbing my eyes, I withdrew from her with a sad smile.

"You have been a good friend. Thank you."

Beautine tried to sign back, but winced, the pain in her hand giving her away.

"Come on," I spoke aloud. "Let's go to the infirmary."

We walked in companionable silence on the way to the infirmary. A few drakes greeted us with a nod or a word. To my surprise, a couple of them even used the sign for hello.

The drakes had enough forethought to keep the infirmary close to the training area. If we'd been at the palace, we'd have to come inside and go up four flights of stairs before winding up and around the tallest tower to get to the physician's study. Even then, he'd lecture you the whole time about taking care of yourself. If he was even available. The majority of the time, we'd find the old coot passed out on a patient's cot, stinking of alcohol.

There weren't many drakes in the infirmary. I'd noticed they heal a lot faster than humans, and most of them didn't even bother to get treated. I knew that Beautine was just humoring me by letting me bring her here. Either way, it made me feel better about my transgression to take care of her.

We found an empty wooden bench to sit on near a worktable. The infirmary was mostly empty except for a few drakes sleeping off last night's revelry.

"Lazy drunks," Beautine said, her eyes rolling at the drakes.

I smiled at her then turned to the supplies on the table.

The drakes didn't follow the same kind of healing procedures as the physician at the palace. They didn't have leeches or weird concoctions that stung the nose and eyes. Everything they had came from the forest or mountain around them. Lavender for pain relief, garlic for a fever. It was different how a race so strong only used such simple things to help them. I'd have said humans were the superior race before meeting them. Now, I've begun to think we might be the ones who should be in hiding.

Picking up a cloth, I wet it in the bowl of water on the table. I turned Beautine's hand over to me, then slowly and carefully cleaned around the edges of the cut. Thankfully, the sword hadn't cut her too deep. I didn't even think it needed stitches.

My eyes focused on the cut as I smoothed the cloth over it and around it. Even after the wound stopped bleeding, I couldn't stop looking at it. My heart raced in my chest, and my head felt foggy. I blinked once, twice, three times, but I couldn't get the sickening feeling in the back of my throat to go away.

Beautine placed her hand on top of mine. Her eyes filled with concern.

I blew out a slow breath, pulling my hands away from her injury and turning to the side. Why was this happening? I'd never had an issue with blood before. The gods know I've seen and cleaned enough of it during my time with Cal and his brother. Why did the blood on Beautine's hand affect me so much?

After a few minutes, Beautine touched my hand.

I slowly turned back to her and found her injured hand covered with the cloth so I couldn't see it. My eyes flicked up to her face, and the pity there made me irrationally angry. I knew she was only worried about me. Beautine had been nothing but nice and understanding. Nothing in her face was saying she thought I was weak or undeserving.

Without a word, I stood and stalked out of the room. I hurried down the corridor, my eyes on my feet and not where I was going. It was no wonder that I didn't run into someone. That would explain why I ended up in the middle of a four-way crossing, completely lost.

Spinning around in place, I tried to figure out which way I'd come from. The markings on the wall weren't much help. I didn't know if I'd come from the east or the west. I'd been so focused on my own pain and self-pitying that I had ended up somewhere I'd never been before.

For a moment, I grew angry, angrier than I had at Beautine's pity. I was angry with myself and my helplessness in this situation with Cal and the drakes. I thought I was being brave and taking his disgusting touch for the sake of my kingdom. Then I thought I had the kingdom's good at heart when I came running to the drakes.

Now... I wasn't so sure.

Did I really run from Cal for the sake of the kingdom or my own?

Was I so broken that I'd fool myself and everyone else into believing that what Cal did didn't bother me? That it was just marks on my body that could be so easily erased once I had Cal's head on a spike?

Unable to handle my own thoughts anymore, I forced myself to start walking. I didn't know where I was going, but the further into the corridor I chose, the more I realized I wasn't going the way I should be. The ground inclined until my calves burned with the exertion it took to get up it.

For some reason, the pain felt good. The more I pushed myself to go up the incline, the clearer my head and lighter my heart felt until I burst forth through the top of the corridor and out into the open air.

My eyes drank up the area around me, not sure where exactly I'd come out of the mountain from, but it wasn't at ground level. The sky seemed closer, the clouds within fingers reach. I edged out onto the grass ledge a bit further until I could just peak over the edge.

The distance up from the ground was so small that I swallowed and stepped back from the edge. Still, I didn't rush back inside. I took a moment to stand there and breathe. Maybe I'd stayed underground too long. It was messing with my head and making everything more intense than it needed to be.

I felt him before he came into my line of sight. Ira may not be the king of the drakes, but he had a presence to him that was hard to ignore. I glanced away from the skyline to the drake prince.

Ira's one good eye crinkled. "Seems you've found my hiding spot."

Chapter 13
Ira

THE SCENT OF the princess filled Ira's senses long before he found her in his secret hiding place. The sharp smell of tears surrounded her, and the heavy stink of despair lingered in the air.

Georgia didn't seem to notice him at first. Her chest heaved, and her fingers curled into fists at her sides.

Her long skirt had been replaced with a shorter skirt, giving her more range of motion in her legs. Her breasts were bound with a strip of fabric covering her from her breastbone to touch the fabric at her waist.

Ira's eyes skimmed over the princess, noticing the way that

fabric covered every inch of where that the Plumus prince had marked. Ira hadn't seen the marks himself, though Ryu had told his brothers about them. Not in much detail but enough to know where they were.

But something had shaken the princess up, her fiery temperament replaced by... this.

In the time she had been with them, Ira had not seen her lose that fire. Any tears had been well calculated from Ryu's point of view.

Suddenly, Ira felt as if he were intruding on a private moment. A quiet moment of desperation where the past clung to the princess's mind, clouding the present with what she had experienced.

Ira knew such moments well. Usually, he followed them with a long binge of ale and women while he wallowed in his self-loathing. It only ended when one or both of his brothers came to drag him out of it with a fight that ended up with all of them in the infirmary.

Ira stepped from where he'd been hiding behind the entrance to the mountain, intent on leaving the princess in peace. Unfortunately, it seemed she was more in tune with her other senses and noticed him immediately.

Putting on a mask of indifference, Ira offered the princess a smile.

"You've found my hiding spot it seems."

It almost seemed as if the princess couldn't see him. As if she were looking straight through him. Then, after a moment, that fog in her eyes dissipated, and the shadows in her gaze only lingered in the background.

Georgia didn't answer him, though he knew she had read his lips. Instead, those pale chestnut orbs turned back to the skyline.

Ira took it as a dismissal and moved to leave. Her voice stopped him.

"How do you handle it?"

Pausing, Ira processed her words, unsure how to respond. There were many things the princess could be referring to. However, the expression on her face could mean only one thing.

Ira stepped back to her side. His good eye focused on the land below them as he prodded at her mind.

There are days when it all seems too much. Those days, the memories overcome every thought and moment.

What do you do on those days?

Ira gave her a lopsided grin. *Get black out drunk or beat up.*

Georgia arched a brow. *And that helps?*

For a time. Ira crossed his arms over his chest. *More than it used to.*

Georgia didn't say anything back. Her face pinched in concentration. Ira was tempted to let her go about her suffering alone as she seemed determined to do.

But something stopped him.

Instead, Ira found himself asking, *What happened?*

Georgia's head swiveled toward him, her brows furrowed. *How do you know something happened?*

The trigger.

Trigger? Georgia cocked her head to the side. *What trigger?*

Ira inclined his head, his hair falling over his bad eye.

It's something that triggered your past. Made it feel like it was happening all over again, and you keep trying to tell yourself it's fine, you're safe, it's not happening anymore, but...

It's like I'm drowning, and I can't pull in a breath. I just keep sinking down further and further, Georgia finished, letting out a shuddering breath. She blinked rapidly, sucking in that air as if it would stave off the pain.

It wouldn't, Ira knew, but he waited anyway.

The air drew quiet and tight until it seemed as if she had forgotten about his question all together. Then she spoke quietly out loud, her voice raspy and low.

"I cut her."

Ira's brow rose. This wasn't what he'd expected. He didn't ask any questions, just let the princess move at her own pace.

We were training, and I couldn't stop thinking about how much I wanted to kill Callahan. How I wanted him to bleed and suffer how he made me. Her hand shoved at her chest, and the anguish on her face caused a feeling Ira'd never felt before.

He wanted to comfort her. To remove that darkness that blotted out the sky and make her the fiery creature who yelled and screamed at him.

And I didn't see Beautine coming. Luckily, she stopped me. Luckily. Georgia breathed a laugh that held so much bitterness, Ira could taste it. *I'm not so sure. She still ended up hurt and bleeding, just like I had.*

Ira was starting to piece the picture together. He knew

Beautine had been training the princess every day, helping her gain confidence and strength.

Beautine might not have suffered the way Ira and the princess had, but the female drake knew something about feeling weak. That's why she had asked permission from Ryu to train the princess. He could see the difference in Georgia even after only a few weeks of training.

Georgia's muscles were more defined. Her figure, which had been tempting enough before, had slimmed and toned, making her a delectable treat to the eyes.

Ira could see how hurting her friend could cause her such anguish. How it might thrust her back into those days where she had bled for someone else.

This isn't the same. Ira reminded her. *It was an accident.*

Georgia's eyes burned with fury as she turned on him. *Don't you think I know that? I've been telling myself that over and over until it's all I can think about and still, the memories won't go away. It's like I'm there on his table all over again.*

Ira stepped forward at the tears trailing down her face, his hand lifted. One glare at him had Ira dropping that hand. Instead, he hardened his features by placing his hands on his hips.

On your knees.

Georgia stared at him. Her brows bunched together, and her lips pursed to the side in such an adorable way that Ira had a hard time holding his stance.

You feel out of control, Ira explained. *I'm going to give it back.*

How does telling me to kneel give me control? That fire burned in her eyes once more, no longer filled with shame.

If you want to stop, say no more and we will stop. I won't do anything you don't want to do.

Georgia stayed at Ira for a long moment as uncertainty played across her face.

I'm still not sure how this will help.

It will, Ira reassured her. *You are the one in control. I am simply an implement of your control.*

Georgia stared at him for a long moment, and he almost thought she'd tell him to fuck off and storm away. However...

"Okay," she said quietly.

Okay, master. Ira corrected her, his gaze boring into her.

Licking her lips, Georgia nodded and then realized I wanted her to say it.

Okay, master.

That one word sent a whoosh of arousal through Ira. He shoved it down, reminding himself this was about her, not him.

Good. Then on your knees, human.

Georgia sank down to the grass before him, her hands on her knees and her eyes on him, waiting for what he'd ask her to do next.

Ira stepped forward, his clawed hand grabbing her jaw just tight enough to pinch.

You've been a bad human, haven't you, princess?

He stroked his other hand over her smooth cheek before cupping the back of her neck, his hand firm as he tilted her head back.

Georgia didn't answer so Ira gave her braided hair a tug.

"Yes," she gasped out.

Ira tugged her braid again. *Yes, what?*

She winced but didn't tell him to stop. A spicy scent just barely susceptible filled his nose.

You like it when I hurt you, don't you? Ira tugged on her hair once more, lifting her slightly by the chin until her knees were barely touching the ground. Georgia groaned in response. Sliding his tongue along the line of her jaw, Ira barely held back a moan as he struggled to give her the next task.

Touch yourself. Ira released her jaw and stepped back so he could watch her.

Georgia's hand moved tentatively, her eyes still wary of

him. Her hand traced along her other arm and across her chest.

Ira jerked on her braid, flashing his fangs at her. *Do not tease, human. You know what I want.*

Blinking up at him, Georgia's hand moved at a mind-numbing pace down her chest, over her abdomen, and then slid her skirt to the side to dip her fingers between her thighs.

The moment she opened her folds enough to slip her fingers in between them, Ira inhaled sharply. She smelled absolutely divine. Ira wanted nothing more than to feast between her legs until she exploded in his mouth.

He couldn't, though. Not yet. This was about her. Teaching her about control.

Do you feel how wet you are, you filthy human whore? Ira growled into her mind, giving her hair an extra tug. *You didn't just come to us for our protection, did you?*

Georgia didn't answer, her fingers still moving between her

thighs, little moans coming from her throat.

Time to turn it up a notch.

Ira's tail swung out and wrapped around Georgia's throat. Her eyes flew open, staring at him in a mixture of shock and terror. He left his tail pulsating around her throat, not squeezing enough so she couldn't breathe but enough that she knew it was there.

Just as he thought, the scent of the princess's arousal spiked in the air. It was so thick it was almost tangible.

By the sounds coming from Georgia, he could tell she was close to coming.

Stop, he commanded.

Georgia kept moving her fingers, not listening to his orders. Ira grabbed her arm and pulled it from between her thighs. The princess stared up at him in confusion, her face pink with arousal, her large breasts heaving with each breath.

When I say, stop. You stop.

For a second, anger filled her eyes, but a tug on her braid reminded her why she was there. Pressing her lips together tight, Georgia nodded.

Ira tugged on her braid again, this time hard enough to make her wince.

The growl that came from her would make any drake proud before she succumbed.

"Yes, master."

Good little whore. Ira released her hand and patted her cheek. *Now open your mouth.*

The defiance in her eyes made him think she wasn't going to do it. Then slowly, as if forcing herself to do it, the princess opened her mouth.

Taste yourself, Ira commanded, knowing she was going to fight it.

Lifting the hand still covered in her drying liquids, Georgia gave him a rude gesture as she slid her fingers between her lips.

Ira smirked at her little act of rebellion. *Suck them clean.*

Georgia's cheeks suctioned in her mouth as she worked her fingers in and out. The image was obscene enough that Ira's already straining cock twitched.

That's a good girl. Now— His thought was interrupted when he caught the scent of someone approaching. His head jerked up, and he released her hair. *Get up. We're done.*

Georgia gaped at Ira, confusion filling her eyes.

Ira stepped back from her and turned on his heel. He disappeared into the foliage lining the side of the mountain, leaving the princess to deal with his brother alone.

Chapter 14

I COULDN'T BELIEVE Ira. that bastard of a drake left me here on my knees, my pride tarnished and my thighs wet with my throbbing arousal. It was my fault for going along with the asinine drake idea. How did I think that letting him order me around would make me stop thinking about my past trauma?

It's not like I liked being down there on my knees, his claws in my hair, with him ordering me to touch myself. No. There was no way I was that fucked up.

Squeezing my eyes shut, I pushed off the ground and brushed off my knees. I turned around and almost stumbled back at the sight of Ryu standing there, watching me with a curious look on his face.

What are you doing out here, pet?

Licking my lips, I put my hands behind my back so he couldn't see me fidgeting.

Nothing. Just got lost and ended up here.

Oh? Ryu strolled forward, his steps languid and teasing. *So why do you smell like you want me to bend you over and fuck you out in the open where everyone can see us?*

Of course he could smell my arousal. Could he smell his brother on me too? He'd only touched my hair and face. But maybe that was enough to let him know Ira was there? Speaking of which, he was a double bastard for leaving me to explain myself to Ryu alone.

Well? Ryu asked again as he wrapped his hands around my waist, his tail sliding up the inside of my thighs.

Before I could protest, the end of his tail flicked against my soaked and aching heat, and all thought of running away to hide my shame of what I did with Ira disappeared.

My hips rocked against the tip of his tail, grinding down on it until I gasped and groaned for more. Ryu grasped me by my backside and lifted me up. My legs wrapped around his waist, eager to feel him inside of me, stretching me as it filled up this need his damn brother left behind.

Ryu shifted his clothing away, the thick head of his cock brushing against the lips of my pussy. I grabbed his shoulder, looking for momentum to push myself down on him. Ryu's chuckle vibrated through me as he thrust his cock into me. He easily slipped in with how wet and ready I was to be taken.

What have you been doing up here, little one? Ryu growled in my head. *You're so hot and wet for me already. Were you thinking about me?*

I cried out and pushed myself down onto his cock again and again, not giving him the answer he was searching for. I couldn't tell him I'd been touching myself for his brother. There was no telling how he would react.

Ryu had made it clear I belonged to him when the other drakes tried to touch me. Did that same courtesy extend to his brothers? Desmond and Ira didn't seem worried their brother would be upset with them for touching me.

To my utter humiliation, I came faster and harder than I ever have in my entire life. Ryu, of course, had no clue that the reason I was so hyped up was because of his brother. Which meant that once my orgasm had torn through me, I felt like the worst person alive.

Scrambling off Ryu, I shoved my clothing back in place, then ran back into the mountain before

Ryu could figure out what was happening.

I didn't stop running until I was out of breath and back near the bottom of the mountain. Thankfully, Ryu nor Ira followed me back down.

Leaning against the wall to catch my breath, I tried to ignore those giving me curious looks on their way by. At least the sight of them meant I was going in the right direction.

By now, I'd gotten over the fact that every single one of them knew from my smell that I'd just been thoroughly fucked by their king. I'd found it resoundingly creepy and embarrassing at first. Then I realized they were more mature than the humans at court who couldn't stop talking about who was fucking who behind their spouse's back. I knew their curious looks had more to do with why I'd been running in the corridor and less about why I smelled of sweat and sex.

My mind now set on a bath, I walked at a slower pace, praying I didn't run into any of the other drake princes. The last thing I needed was to run into Desmond and have him tease me. The way things were going right now, I'd likely bend over and let him clean me up himself.

The very thought made me press my thighs together. Shame burned my face, and I shook my head. I needed to get it together. The future of my kingdom was at stake. I couldn't let my desire ruin this for them.

I stopped by the king's room to get a change of clothes before heading toward the royal hot spring. I could bathe in the female's quarters, but that would mean seeing Beautine, and I wasn't ready for that yet. At least, the only ones I was likely to run into at the royal hot spring were the princes and their king. The likelihood of that happening at this time of day was quite low.

Ryu would normally be in meetings with either his brothers or his council, planning on how we would take Callahan and his brother down. When not meeting with them, Ryu would tend to the needs of his people. Who, despite their seeming simplicity, had as many problems as my own court.

Hoping this was one of those times they were all busy, I rounded the corner and found the hot spring occupied by my very own handmaiden and... Desmond?

I blinked, not believing what I was seeing. They weren't bathing or even doing anything unsavory that I'd need to wash my eyes out. In fact, I didn't know what they were doing.

Aryn sat across from Desmond on the ground just off to the side of the hot spring. The handmaiden had the drake prince's hands in hers, moving them into a certain position before shifting them to another. Desmond watched with keen interest, memorizing every movement, his tail tapping against the ground behind him like a happy dog.

Too far away to read her lips, I couldn't understand what Aryn was telling him or Desmond's response. They continued the hand movements for a few more minutes before I realized it.

That traitor was teaching them to sign!

Teaching my guard to sign was one thing but the princes' who already had an all access pass to my mind was another.

No longer feeling the need to hide, I stepped out and into the hot spring. Desmond noticed me first even though his back was to me. Turning around, he smiled at me and greeted me with his hands.

"Hello, how are you?"

I bared my teeth at him, pouring all my anger and frustration into my glare. Then I signed several things I knew he wouldn't know for sure but still make it blatantly obvious that I was mad at him.

Aryn gaped at my signs, jumped to her feet, and grabbed my hands. Shaking her head at me, she twisted her head around and said something to Desmond before giving me a disapproving look.

"Upset or not," Aryn signed to me, her patience clear in her movements, "there is no need for such language. If you are upset with me, you need to tell me, not to take it out on the prince who only wanted to make you feel more at home."

I stared at her hands and then to her face before glancing shyly over at Desmond who watched our exchange with great interest. Had he really been trying to learn sign language so I'd feel more comfortable?

"How do I know they aren't learning it to spy on us?" I signed back to Aryn with a frown.

Aryn smiled and gestured to Desmond to come over to us. As he came close, she signed slowly so he could keep up.

"Tell her what you told me."

Desmond paused.

I could practically see the wheels turning in his head as he thought about how to respond. I had to admit, I was curious to see how far along they had gotten in their lessons. How had I not known they were working on this? Did the others know how to sign as well now?

I was both happy and irritated by that prospect.

Desmond moved his hands, his signs unsure and sloppy but clear enough I could understand him.

"Ira suggested we learn to sign to help you feel more at home here. We want you to be able to stand up for yourself." He paused once more, glancing at Aryn. She nodded her encouragement. "Like at the market."

My cheeks warmed at his words, not knowing what to say. No one had bothered to learn for my benefit.

They learned at the palace because I was the princess and

they had to. Aryn learned because it was part of her job. My father learned because what other choice did he have? These drakes had no reason to learn my language other than to use it against me or... if what Desmond is saying is true, to make me feel more at home.

At a loss for words, I did the only thing I could. I pressed my fingers to my lips and pushed them toward him.

"Thank you."

Chapter 15
Desmond

A WEEK AFTER the incident with Georgia, Desmond along with three other scouts, prowled the Gebe forest. Normally, they would send whole troops out to check the surrounding areas for trespassers, but with the Plumus prince searching for his betrothed, it just wasn't safe for so many of the drakes to be out of the mountain. The fewer at risk, the better.

Desmond had to argue with his brother just for Ryu to let him go on patrol.

"It'll be fine," Desmond had reassured him. "I've done this a thousand times."

"Yes, but this time they are actively looking for us, not just hoping they wander upon our camp," Ryu had shot back with much more ferocity than Desmond had expected.

"We will be going under the cover of night. No one sees better in the dark than the drakes." Desmond patted his brother on the back. "You just take care of the princess and leave the enemies to me."

Now slipping through the forest in the dead of night, even the moon had hidden itself as if to aid their cause, Desmond wondered what all the fuss had been about. Neither he nor his males had seen hide or hair of the prince's soldiers. Not even the wayward set of guards the king of Kinoko sent out every once in a while to keep thieves from using the forest road for their victims.

"This is pointless," Bak, the young drake to Desmond's right groaned. The red-scaled youth picked at his claws and dragged his fingers across his horns. "Why are we even out here? There's nothing and no one here."

Nabaliv, the brownish orange scaled drake next to him smacked the youngling over the head. "Just because you don't see them doesn't mean they do not exist. All your whining will draw the humans right to us."

"And we don't want that, right?" Bak asked as he scratched the side of his face with a claw.

"No," Desmond answered him simply. "We don't."

"But the princess is a human..." Bak continued, and Desmond knew where he was going with this.

"Not all humans are our enemies," Desmond explained, keeping his ears open for any movement around them. "Some, like the Kinokos, need our help. While others, like the Plumus, want to destroy us. Those are who we are looking for."

"But how do we know which is which?" Bak whined.

Something snapped to the east.

"Quiet." Desmond put his hand up.

"They all look the same, you know? All fleshy and hairy," Bak continued as if Desmond hadn't spoken.

A whistling hurtled toward them, and Desmond moved. Throwing himself at the youngling, he knocked Bak out of the way, but sharp pain registered in the prince's side.

"To the east," Nabaliv called to their other companion, while Desmond dislodged the arrow in his side. His scales had kept the tip of the arrow from going too far in but it still stung and bled quite a bit.

Desmond pulled himself to his feet with a wince, and he withdrew his machete from his back.

"Oh, by the gods, Your Highness," Bak cried out, trying to wrap his arms around the prince. "You saved me. How can I ever thank you?"

Desmond pried the male off him and grabbed the youth by the

shoulders. "You can stop talking and start killing. This is the time you prove yourself, Bak. Alright?"

Bak nodded vigorously, grabbed his bow off his back, and nocked an arrow.

Confident the young one would find his way, Desmond turned his attention to the fight at hand.

About a dozen soldiers were closing in on them. It didn't matter to him what banner they bore. Since they struck first, Desmond didn't care if the princess cared for them. He'd not let them hurt him or his comrades.

Nabaliv fought off three of them, swinging his claymore around like it was as light as a feather. He cut two of them in half, knocking the third back to scramble away.

Desmond didn't know where his other companion went until a loud cry came from the sky and the small dark-scaled drake barreled into a group of soldiers. Knocking them down with the might of his hammer to the ground, she swung it around in a whirlwind keeping any who might come at her back.

Several of the humans had decided to come after Desmond and Bak. Desmond swung his machete, knocking them back while Bak shot at them.

For a loudmouth youngling, Bak wasn't a bad shot. Twice he hit a soldier that was about to get Desmond in the back.

Once the soldiers were either dead or incapacitated Desmond checked the surrounding trees for any others.

"Do you see anything?" Bak whisper-yelled at him.

Desmond shook his head and then grinning from ear to ear, he turned to Bak. "You did a great job. I knew you could do it."

"Your Highness!" Bak's dark brown eyes widened. "Watch out!"

Before Bak could get an arrow nocked, pain laced into Desmond's back. He swiped his tail behind him, taking the soldier out before falling to his knees.

The battle must have been over because the others rushed to his side. Nabaliv checked the spot where the dagger still lived in Desmond's flesh. Desmond grunted and pushed Nabaliv's hands away.

"We need to pull it out and bind it. Then we can take care of it back at the infirmary." Nabaliv pulled something out of the small bag at his waist. "Here. Chew on this. It will help with the pain."

"Pain? What pain?" Desmond huffed a laugh. "I'm perfectly fine." He pushed himself to his feet, and the world tipped sideways and then everything went black.

When Desmond woke, there was a lot of commotion happening around him. Laying on his front, Desmond found himself atop one of the infirmary cots with the taste of copper in his mouth.

"Bring me clean water," Nabaliv ordered to someone else while he did something to Desmond's back.

Desmond couldn't feel what the drake was doing to him. There was pressure, but nothing definitive. He should be able to feel it.

"Did you drug me?" Desmond asked, his words coming out slow and slurred.

"You bet your tail I did," Nabaliv commented, shifting to the side so that Desmond could see him. "And if you get stubborn, I'll drug you again."

Desmond wanted to argue, but his head felt heavy, and his eyes drifted back closed.

When he opened them again, it was quiet. Desmond still laid on one of the infirmary cots, his chest down. He tried to shift to roll over, but the movement pulled at something in his back, making him hiss.

"Don't do that."

Desmond searched for the owner of the voice he'd come to look forward to every day.

Georgia sat on a chair beside his cot, a long piece of cloth spread over her legs. It looked as if she'd been mending it.

The infirmary was quiet. They must have cleared it out for him which in itself annoyed him. He didn't need special treatment.

Desmond moved to try to sign her.

Rest. Her voice pushed into his thoughts. *Don't strain yourself on my account. You've done enough saving for today.*

The others... are they...?

Georgia smiled putting her project down to lean over him. A cool cloth slid over the side of his face. *They're fine. Just some scrapes and bruises. You're the only fool who came back on death's bed.* She poked his cheek with a frown.

Desmond watched her face, searching for what he didn't know.

I worried you.

Looking at him through her lashes, Georgia went back to wiping his face with a cloth.

Can you blame me? You went out to fight for my cause and came back injured. Of course, I was worried.

Because if I was dead then Ryu would be less likely to help you, Desmond prodded, trying to see if he could get her to admit how she really felt.

Georgia pursed her lips together. *No. Because if you died, I'd have one less drake to fight against Callahan, and I need as many of you as I can get.*

Her words would have annoyed Desmond if not for the small smile playing on her lips. He wouldn't push her anymore. Not right now at least. Desmond wanted her to pamper him more. If he pushed her too far, he knew she'd leave.

They sat there without speaking for a long moment. Georgia gave him water slowly from a cup which was awkward laying on his front. He ended up spilling most of it down his chin.

Did you find out who those soldiers belonged to? Desmond asked at last.

Georgia worked at cleaning up the mess and grimaced. *They were a mix of Callahan's and my father's soldiers. Which, believe me, the very thought of it has my stomach in knots.*

Desmond pushed up on his forearms ignoring the pain.

What does it mean?

Georgia lifted her eyes to meet his, her distress coming through in her thoughts. *It means something has happened at home. Something bad.*

Chapter 16

IT'D BEEN SEVERAL days since Desmond came back bloodied and unconscious. I'd stopped by to check on him every day, even going so much as to sit with him during meals much to his annoyance.

Walking down the corridor, I let my fingers trail across the dirt walls, letting the cool feel of it soothe me while I fought with my inner turmoil. I'd just finished with him a few minutes ago, where the healer and I fought to keep him from trying to get up yet.

When Desmond's patrol party had come back with him injured, I didn't know what to think. My heart raced in my chest, and a sense of helplessness came over me. I still felt that way even though I did my part just now.

Desmond got hurt because of me. The sweet drake who'd gone out of his way to help me with the marketplace and even convinced went out of his way to learn sign for me. Sure, he liked to tease me and push the boundaries of what was proper but that didn't mean I wanted him hurt or killed.

Of course, I should have known this would happen. I'd come to the drakes for their help after all. I should have known that it would mean they would get hurt in the process. Some would even, I swallowed at the thought, die.

Coming to them had been a rash plan that I hadn't thought all the way through, even though I'd told Aryn I had. A part of me wished we'd never come here in the first place.

I hadn't thought of the drakes who would put their lives on the line for me. Or that I would come to care about some of them and even befriend them. That made their sacrifice even harder to swallow. I'd only been thinking about my pain and my people.

You're doing it again.

I jerked and spun around, finding the source of the voice in my head.

Scowling at the one eye drake, I pushed past Ira and walked toward the baths.

Desmond doesn't regret fighting for you. You should stop blaming yourself for it.

I twisted around to face him. "I'm not," I snarled. "Go away."

Ira's shadow fell over me, not caving to my demands. *If you keep beating yourself up about it, Desmond will only feel worse about getting hurt. He really is far too noble for a drake. He probably would have made a great knight in your castle.*

I tried my best to ignore Ira's words in my head, but they made me think what it would be like to have the drakes in the castle.

Outwardly, the ladies would all be appalled, but on the inside, they'd be leering at the exposed scaled muscles and daydreaming about the large bulge between their legs. That was until the ladies realized the drakes used those tails of theirs for other things than battle and balance.

Giggling to myself, I caught the smirk on Ira's face. With a huff, I turned away and faced forward. I picked up my pace, hoping to discourage him from following me. Sadly, even when I reached the hot springs, I hadn't deterred him. Spinning on my heel, I poked a finger at his chest.

I want to bathe. So do me a favor and find someone else to annoy.

Ira glanced down at her, his eyes heating.

Go ahead. I'm not stopping you.

Your mere presence is a disturbance.

Stepping closer to me, Ira reached up — I froze, afraid of what he would do and almost salivating with what he might — except he only brushed a bit of my hair behind my ear.

Are you saying you did not enjoy our last session?

I shivered against his claws scraping along my cheek. To my horror, desire pooled between my thighs. Licking my lips, I shoved away from him with a glare at his smirking face.

No. It was wrong. I'm with... I belong to Ryu. Not you.

Ira's brow arched. *Is that your only argument? That you belong to my brother? I was under the understanding that you were a person and belonged to yourself. Perhaps I was mistaken, and you are a broken toy after all.*

That I knew he was just trying to rile me up didn't stop me from shoving his chest and snarling.

You know what I mean; I made a deal with Ryu. I cannot go back on my side of the bargain, or all of this will be for nothing.

So your only objection is that you have made a deal with my brother to save your kingdom? Remind me, what was the deal exactly? Ira's eyes traced over my form, lingering on the junction between my thighs which were pressed tightly together. He inhaled deeply which only caused me to squirm more.

I... I offered myself to the king for the drake's help against Plumus.

Ira's lips twitched. *That was not the arrangement.*

Frowning at the drake, I thought back to the beginning. I'd been on my knees before the king with Aryn. They wanted to know why we were there. Why shouldn't they kill them for trespassing? Then I told Aryn to offer me to the king so they wouldn't kill us...

Returning my attention to the drake before me, I scowled.

I may not have offered myself for help but I offered myself to Ryu so you wouldn't kill us. So, there. Keep your hands to yourself.

Ira wrapped a strand of my hair around his finger and stared at it.

You may not know what your handmaiden said, but I do. She didn't offer you to the king directly.

Aryn offered you to the drakes in return for safety. Drakes, plural. Meaning if I wanted to strip you down and make you grab your ankles while I buried my face in your delicious smelling cunt, then I could.

My mouth dropped open, and Ira traced the line of my lips before dipping that finger into my mouth. Against my will, my tongue swiped out to taste his skin, his claw scraping against the tip of my tongue.

Was that true? Had Aryn really said that? I had no way to be certain without confronting her directly and then I'd have to explain why exactly I wanted to know. Which would lead to what I'd been doing with Ira.

I could scream for him to go away. Stand on my righteous hill of 'I belong to the king.' I could…

But I wouldn't.

Some part of me wanted this. If the ache between my thighs wasn't enough proof, a fundamental part of me, something lodged in my chest, said I needed this. What Ira had to offer.

Doing this, though... doing this knowing that I shouldn't meant I couldn't turn around and say Ira had coerced or forced me to do it. None of this had ever been about forcing me. The drake prince had told me this was about control. My own control and my willingness to give it to him.

No. I'd be doing this because I wanted to and for no other reason. I just hoped Ryu didn't punish me for it. Swallowing, I closed my mouth and pushed my thoughts at him.

Then why don't you?

Releasing my chin, Ira stepped back a step. *Take your clothes off.*

Pulling my lower lip between my teeth, I untied the red silken material around my neck, letting it drop to the ground. That bared my breasts to him, as well as most of my scars.

For some reason, I wasn't worried about Ira seeing my scars. With Ryu. I'd been worried he'd be disgusted by what he saw when I finally revealed them. With Ira... it was like I was showing him my true self. Something he already accepted and wanted, even with the scars. Because Ira had his own.

Ira's eyes drifted along the swell of my breasts and lingered on my nipples before sliding down to my waist. They didn't linger on the scars or so much as flinch over them. Instead, he almost had a look of awe on his face, his fingers tracing along the edge of the bottom half of my clothing.

Untying the bottom half, I breathed out as I released it. Standing bare before the drake prince, I waited with bated breath for him to tell me what to do.

When those eyes lifted back to mine, Ira let out his command.

"On your hands and knees."

Chapter 17
Ira

GEORGIA'S SCENT OF arousal spiked in the air, letting Ira know exactly how much she wanted this as she lowered herself down to the ground.

Do you remember what to say when you want me to stop? Ira asked, circling the princess's kneeling form.

Pulling her lower lip between her teeth, Georgia nodded.

That wouldn't do.

Ira smacked her on one ass cheek, causing her to squeak, but she didn't move from her position.

You must say it. I need to know you know what to do when it's too much.

Georgia panted, her need almost palpable. *No more.*

Good girl. Ira stroked her hair as he passed by.

If the princess had turned around and told him to leave, he'd have done so right then. Ira knew she wouldn't, though. She wanted this too badly. Needed it.

Ira knew all about the need for control.

He'd been on the wrong side of it for a long time. It took him years to get to where he could top someone else. Ira had been in the princess's place for a long time, fighting for that piece of himself that he couldn't dislodge.

Ira wanted nothing more than to help the princess deal with her pain. She needed it if she was planning to face down her abuser. If she didn't quell the shadows inside of her when she came face to face with her betrothed once again, she'd freeze up, the same way that Ira did.

Ira almost touched his eye at that thought, but he forced his hand down to his side. Now was not the time to linger on old scars. Not when such a bountiful meal laid out before him, ready for the tasting.

Spread your legs wider. Ira commanded, walking around her until he could see her pale pink folds, dripping with her arousal. Oh, how Ira wanted to bury his cock in her and pound into her until they were both shattered and sated. He resisted the urge, he needed to go slow with the princess.

Kneeling behind her, he cupped her hips in his hands, taking care of his claws, before lifting her up so he could reach that intoxicating scent coming from her pussy. The princess arched up onto her toes, her hips pushed back toward him almost eagerly.

For a moment, Ira breathed in the smell of her, the musty feminine scent that had his mouth watering and his cock stirring. Ira's tongue snaked out, and the forked edges of it tickled along her lips, lapping up a few drops of her essence.

Georgia let out a small, startled cry.

Testing the waters a bit more, Ira slipped his long tongue between her folds sliding it up and around her clit before bringing it back down and circling her puckered hole. The way the princess jerked and moaned at his movements only encouraged Ira to keep going.

Instead of diving into her dripping cunt, Ira trailed his tongue along the inside of her thighs, lingering on the place where his brother had marked her.

My brother has marked you. Shall I do so as well? The question was meant to be teasing, but the way her arousal rose at his words made Ira reconsider it.

It wasn't unheard of for more than one drake to mark a female. Their culture was all about the female's will since there were so few of them. Many of the females took multiple partners, while the males for the most part enjoyed their time with them. True mates, where only one mated another, were rare for the drakes. The practicality of taking multiple partners to increase the chances of offspring was something they all understood.

However, the thought of someone other than his brothers touching this smooth peach skin, tasting the delicious cream dripping onto his tongue, caused Ira to growl. Placing a hand on her stomach to keep her lifted, Ira used his other hand to rub furious circles around her clit until she was screeching and jerking in his hold. Just before she could come, Ira bit down, right next to his brother's mark.

Georgia cried out and came, her essence coating his face and tongue while he laved at his mark. She tried to wiggle away from him, but Ira held onto her, smacking one cheek with a resounding smack.

Calm yourself.

The princess turned her head as far as she could to glare at him over her shoulder.

You fucking bit me!

Licking the mark one more time, Ira smirked. *Yes, I did. Now everyone will know who you belong to.*

Georgia's heart rate picked up, and she fought against Ira's hold with more vigor. He released her legs and placed a hand on her back, holding her down against the ground while she huffed and growled like the best of dragons.

"Let me go," she snarled aloud, her nails digging into the dirt floor and glowering at him.

Ira cocked his head to the side. *What do you say?* he reminded her.

Georgia blinked at him for a moment, her thoughts whirling behind her chestnut-colored orbs. Ira hoped she wouldn't say it. They'd just gotten started, and he wanted to play with her some more. However, if she did, Ira would find company with his own hand and let her go.

Apparently, Georgia agreed with him. Instead of saying the words, she shifted on her knees and grunted.

Don't bite me anymore.

Ira gave her a fang-toothed grin. *Into the water.*

Watching Georgia do anything naked was a sight to behold. Even the act of sitting up and sliding into the pool made him anxious to have her.

The princess hissed as the water touched the fresh bite on her thigh. Ira would feel bad about her pain if it didn't need cleaning. Besides, he had other plans for her. A little discomfort would be well worth it.

Shifting around, Ira threw his legs over the side of the pool, the water up to his knees. His tail dipped into the water, making lazy circles nearby.

Georgia eyed him, waiting for her next command.

Such a good girl.

Spreading his thighs wide, Ira crooked a claw at her. *Come here.*

Licking her lips, Georgia swept her arms through the water, bringing herself to sit between Ira's thighs. Her gaze darted from his face to the bulge beneath his clothes and back again. The eagerness of that gaze made Ira wonder how much experience she'd had with his brother's cock.

Untying the loincloth covering his length, Ira wrapped a hand around it, stroking it up and down while the princess watched.

Ira knew his cock wasn't the same as a human's. Drakes were much larger and thicker than any human male's. There was also the aspect of the ridges along their cock, almost like scales except they didn't come up off the skin. Female drakes were used to the feel of it, but humans... Ira was curious to see how the princess would react when he was deep inside her.

Give me your hand.

Georgia eagerly held her hand out to Ira. He took it and replaced one of his own with hers. He moved his hand on top of hers and guided it up and down his shaft, showing her just how he liked to be touched, until she got the rhythm. A quick study, Georgia took over within just a few moments.

Ira leaned back on his hands, letting her touch him as much as she wanted before he was close to the edge. Stopping her by grabbing her hair with one hand,, Ira wrapped her braid around his fist and tugged her forward.

Open up.

Not needing more than that, Georgia leaned forward and scrapped the flat of her tongue across the head of his cock. Ira grunted, holding back from shoving himself completely into her mouth and down her throat. He didn't know how much she could take just yet, and he didn't want to damage his new toy.

Georgia needed no such care. She wrapped a hand around the base of him and shifted until she could take him completely into her mouth. The dirty princess's throat constricted around his cock, squeezing it just so that Ira was already close to the edge once more.

Wanting to cum inside the princess the first time, Ira jerked on her braid to tell her to stop. Georgia's eyes flipped open, defiance shining in them as she took him and sucked him down even harder.

Before Ira could reprimand her for her disobedience, his hips thrust up from the ground as hot cum poured out of him and down her throat. There was so much cum that it dripped out the sides of the princess's mouth. When he was done, the princess pulled back with a satisfied grin on her face, sliding her thumb over the edges of her lips to lick the remnants off.

Ira grabbed her by the chin and pulled her forward until their faces were close together.

You're going to pay for that. Then he smashed his lips onto hers. Ira shoved his tongue into her mouth and licked up all the remaining evidence of him inside of her.

Dropping into the water, Ira flipped their positions, pressing Georgia up against the side of the pool. His hand on her back pushed her down until her face touched the dirt and stone beneath her.

Leaning over her, Ira traced his long tongue along the shell of her ear and murmured into mind.

I hope you're ready for me, princess. Because there's no going back now.

Chapter 18

WHAT WAS WRONG with me? If Cal had put me in this position, pressed down into the dirt, my nipples scraping against the ground, unable to move or fight back, I'd have a panic attack. Why did having Ira treat me like a doll arouse me so much?

My hips arched on their own, shoving my butt toward him. There was something about Ira that set my blood on fire. It wasn't the same as with Ryu, who had completely ruined me for humans. It was just... different. Ira understood me, what I needed more than even I did.

It was a bit unsettling.

The tip of Ira's cock rubbed back and forth against my folds, taking a moment to soak in my juices. Then, without warning, Ira pressed completely inside of me.

I gasped at the intrusion.

Feeling deliciously stretched, my fingers dug into the ground below me. Ira thrust in slow, punishing movements, taking his time to stretch me to fit him. Toe curling ripples of pleasure scoured through me with each thrust, water splashing against my legs and butt with every thrust.

That's my good little whore, Ira grunted in my head. *You like being taken like this, don't you? Unable to move. All you can do is take me in like a good little whore.*

Each filthy word that fluttered through my mind heightened my arousal, sending me up to that edge, teetering on it but not quite going over yet.

I needed something else. Something more.

Something slithered along my leg under the water, creeping its way between me and the side of the pool. The rough tip of Ira's tail flicked at my clit, circling it before roughly rubbing the sensitive bundle of flesh.

That extra stimulation was what I needed to be pushed over the edge. My hands reached and scrabbled for something to hold on to, something to help me through the intensity of the orgasm ripping through my body.

Ira's hand wrapped around my throat, pulling me back against his chest, and I gripped his bicep with both hands, digging my nails into his arm until they broke skin. Still, Ira didn't relent, pounding into me, hitting the end of my inside. The sharp sting only pushed me further into the explosion until I thought I couldn't take it anymore.

Then Ira's chest rumbled against my back, and air rushed by my head in what I guessed was a roar. Hot semen filled me, warming my insides and making my muscles languid and spent.

Releasing me, Ira patted me on the head before pulling back.

Good girl, you did such a good job.

A shudder went through me as I tried to regain my breath on the ground. Ira pet me until I closed my eyes and sighed. Licking my lips, I pushed myself onto my hands, preparing to wash off the evidence of our fucking.

The ground vibrated under my knees, and Ira stilled behind me.

Jerking my head up, my eyes widened at Desmond's smirking form in the doorway.

"I wondered how long it would be before you took her." Desmond's lips moved slowly, his hands moving with each word. "You always wanted what wasn't yours, brother."

Trapped between the horror of being caught by the other drake prince and the annoyance of seeing him out of bed after I'd fought so hard to keep him there, I settled for saying nothing at all.

I shoved myself off the ground and into the water. Ducking beneath the surface, my face burned with shame and humiliation.

What had I been thinking? Why did I think it was okay for me to do this with Ira? Now, Desmond was going to tell Ryu and then everything was going to hell.

To my dismay, my lungs demanded I breath and I had to pop my head back above the surface.

Come, princess, Desmond purred in my head, his hand signs a bit sloppy and unsure. *I won't bite. But it seems as if my brother already did.* He smirked, making my face heat with embarrassment. *I have to say I'm feeling a bit left out.*

I didn't know how the bastard knew that Ira had bitten me with me being in the water, but I wasn't about to let this drake prince bite me for the sake of fairness.

Ira didn't seem bothered or hadn't heard his brother's words. He only treaded water beside me, his lips ticked up in a self-satisfied grin.

Glaring at Desmond, I shot him a rude gesture. That caused him to laugh and hold his hands up.

Not to worry, princess. I know when I'm not wanted. I'll just have to work harder to win you over. He winked before disappearing out the door.

Ira shifted through the water, ripples following him in his wake as he closed in on me. My eyes didn't soften as he approached, something that he noticed by the way his smile dropped. My shoulders curled into myself, and I pushed back from him.

What's wrong? He didn't reach for me, keeping his distance and hands to himself. *Are you regretting what we did?*

I didn't. Not really. My insides still tingled from what we did, and I couldn't find it in myself to hate it. I did worry, though.

Will he tell Ryu? I blinked, trying not to let my frustration at the whole situation take over. If or when, the more likely of the two, Ryu found out, would it affect the drake king's promise to help me against Callahan?

Ira had assured me that it was alright. That Ryu wouldn't care that I belonged to all the drakes, not just the king. Or rather, whatever drake I decided to be with. I didn't think they would force me to bed all of them, not if I didn't want to.

Moving a bit closer, Ira lifted his hand and brushed his fingers against my cheek. It was gentle, so much in contrast to his savage love making that it startled me.

Desmond is a lot of things, but he is no gossip. Still...

I froze at the word. *Still what?*

Ira shifted into my space, his hands coming to rest on my waist. *I do believe Ryu should know. Letting him find out on his own will not bode well with him. Our king favors honesty above all else.*

Chewing on my lip, I nodded. I wasn't sure I agreed with Ira, but what else was I going to do? Ryu would see the mark Ira placed on me next to his the next time we had sex, so I couldn't hide it from him for long.

Question was, how did I tell my sort of master that I let his brother violate me and I liked it... a lot?

Chapter 19
Ryu

THE DRAKE KING leaned over the map of the five kingdoms, his eyes on the map before him but not really seeing it. The Plumus troops were moving on the border of Kinoko. There'd been reports of large numbers of them creeping along the edges, a little at a time coming through the border. How they managed to get across the border without the Kinoko king finding out, Ryu didn't know. Or perhaps Fergus did know and let the Plumus prince bring in more troops to find his princess?

Either way, Ryu wasn't thinking about how to stop the troops or what it would mean for the drakes. His mind was centered around one voluptuous princess who he hadn't seen in three days.

It wouldn't be unusual if they didn't share a room. Each night, Georgia was asleep before he came to the room and then gone in the morning, even before him.

Ryu didn't know if she was escaping to the female's quarters or training with Beautine. If he went to either place, she made sure to be gone before Ryu appeared. There was no way it was a coincidence that he missed her every time. Which only meant one thing.

Georgia was avoiding him.

The question Ryu couldn't answer was why? Had he done something to upset her? Or perhaps he'd forgotten to do something and that was what she avoided him?

"You look deep in thought, brother." Desmond's voice came from behind him as he walked into the war room. "The plans giving you troubles?"

Ryu grunted in response.

How would he explain to his brother that the little human woman was causing him distress? It was hardly drake-like to be so worried about his place with someone, especially a relationship that was supposed to be a means to an end. They were together simply because of their mutual cause against the Plumus, not because they had fallen for each other.

Technically, Ryu could have ended the first arrangement they had made – the princess's body for her and the handmaiden's life – now that they had a different sort of arrangement.

Ryu would be lying if he said he didn't enjoy their time together. He'd never found someone so responsive to his touch, so eager to take his cock in any orifice he wanted, even if that meant she didn't come in return. Not that Ryu had allowed that to happen. It was a matter of pride to make the human princess scream and squeal her release, digging her nails into any part of his body she could grab a hold of. He had crescent shaped markings on his scales to prove it.

Ryu hadn't asked for anything in return for his help against Plumus, though there was an unspoken agreement. Ryu had assumed if they proceeded with this tentative truce, they would become allies after the Plumus issue was resolved.

Now... Ryu wasn't so sure.

Maybe Georgia was keeping her distance because she wanted to break off their previous agreement?

A stinging thwomp hit his head, and Ryu spun around with a snarl.

"What was that for?"

Desmond smirked. "I was saying your name, and you never answered me." His lips turned down into a frown. "This must really be bothering you if you're thinking that hard on it."

Turning back to the map, Ryu sighed. "It's not the Plumus

troops. Though we do need to get a headcount and figure out how they are getting in without the king protesting. I don't think Fergus would let himself be put in such a vulnerable position voluntarily."

"I agree." Desmond bobbed his head. "If it's not Plumus, then what's bothering you."

Ryu didn't answer, unsure how to explain what he was feeling.

Desmond leaned against the edge of the table, his tail smacking the ground next to them. "Maybe a certain human female who has certainly caused quite a stir around here?"

Ryu grunted in answer.

"Ah, so it is because of the princess. I should have known." Desmond chuckled, shaking his head. "What did she do now?"

"She's avoiding me. That's what."

Desmond frowned. "Are you sure? Maybe you're just coming and going at different times?"

Ryu's hand curled around a wooden figure on the table, the edges of it biting into his palm.

"I'm sure of it. There's no other explanation."

Nodding, Desmond hummed. "Well, if you don't think you caused any reason for her to avoid you, I would ask her. Better yet... ask Ira."

Ryu's head jerked up at the suggestion. "Why should I ask him?"

The door to the war room opened, and the very brother they were talking about walked in.

"Ah, speak of the drake." Desmond pointed his tail in the direction of his brother. "Ira, our dear king wants to know why his princess is avoiding him. Do you know anything about that?"

Brows pinched together, Ryu watched the expression on Ira's face shift from pleasant to completely blank. Which only meant he was hiding something. Ryu's tail slapped the ground in an agitated rhythm.

"Well, brother? What say you?"

Ira cocked his head to the side, blinking at him as he gave nothing away. "She didn't tell you?"

Teeth grinding together, Ryu stepped toward the drake. "Tell me what?"

Striding languidly up to the table, Ira studied the map with feigned interest. He stroked his jaw, humming under his breath while picking up one wooden piece off the table and placing it elsewhere.

The asshole was doing this on purpose, dragging out the answers that Ryu so desperately wanted.

"Do not test me, brother. If you know something, explain," Ryu growled, stalking around the table to invade his brother's side.

Ira turned his head so that his good eye faced Ryu, still not showing any urgency to explain to Ryu what was going on with the human princess.

"I'm not sure I should tell you. If the princess didn't deign to explain what is wrong, then maybe she didn't want you to know?"

Without warning, Ryu grabbed his brother by the throat and jerked him away from the table. Ira clashed his horns on his head against Ryu's, snarling back at him with as much aggression as Ryu.

"You may be my brother, but I am your king. You will answer me when I ask you a question." Ryu pushed against his brother's head, reminding him of who was dominant of the two of them.

Ira snort-laughed and swung his tail out, smacking Ryu on the back of the knees and sending them both tumbling to the ground. Desmond, the bastard, watched from the sidelines amused by their squabbling.

Wrapping his arms around his brother's neck and head, Ryu held him in a head lock, his legs pinning Ira's in place.

"Do you yield?"

Gasping through the pressure Ryu placed on his throat, Ira grunted, "Fine. I yield."

Ryu released him, and they both climbed to their feet.

Calmly taking his place by the table once more, Ryu waited for his brother to catch his breath before interrogating him further.

"What do you know?" he finally asked.

Ira rubbed his neck and grimaced. "I think you bruised my windpipe."

Ryu snarled a warning.

"You are more impatient than a babe waiting for his mother's milk," Ira commented with a shake of his head. Sighing, Ira kept his eyes on Ryu as he continued. "The princess is likely avoiding you because she doesn't know how to explain to you that we have mated."

Ryu's brows shot up.

Of all the reasons the princess could be avoiding him, Ryu hadn't expected that answer. It did make sense though. Georgia probably thought that she had violated their arrangement by having sex with his brother. Something they had never specified, but seeing as she was human, she didn't quite have the same mindset as the drakes when it came to sexual partners.

"I see," Ryu murmured, stroking his jaw with his fingers. "And when did this occur?"

Ira shrugged. "A few days ago. Though we did have a session a bit before that up on the cliff. You interrupted us."

"Ah, that was the scent I smelled on her before."

Ira inclined his head in response.

It all made sense now. The princess's avoidance, the extra scent on her person that seemed familiar but he couldn't put his finger on it. Ryu had just thought it was from training, but if Georgia and Ira were bedding one another, that made more sense. With the mystery solved, Ryu turned his attention back to the map before him.

"The Plumus troops are coming in from the far east side of the southern border, they have at least two thousand men. If the Kinoko king knows about it, he isn't stopping them."

"My spies are getting me more information," Ira added, unbothered by Ryu's change of subject. "From what they have learned so far from sneaking around the troops planted outside the castle, the Plumus princes are now in charge. Whether that means they have killed the king or not remains to be seen."

Ryu huffed. "Then we should plan for an all-out war." Turning to Desmond, Ryu commanded, "Send out messenger birds to the drakes in the Boyon mountains. If the Plumus princes plan to attack us with the full force of their arm, then we are going to need as much help as we can get."

Desmond winced. "Are you sure? Those Gunni drakes are a bit volatile. I blame the wings.

They have to be suffering from oxygen loss from flying too high."

"Regardless," Ryu stared at the map, his eyes on the castle in the middle of Kinokos, "we need them. Who knows what will happen after Plumus takes over Kinoko? Gunni could be next, and we have to be prepared."

Chapter 20

SITTING NEXT TO aryn in the female's quarters, she signed something about what happened with the male drakes but I wasn't really paying attention. My fingers twisted and turned into the edges of my skirt.

For days now, I felt on edge. Every shadow made me jump. Every drake close to the color of the king made me run. It almost felt as if I was back in the castle, trying to hide from Cal and Luis. Except I was hiding from Ryu for a whole different reason.

While Ira had assured me that Ryu wouldn't care that we had been with one another, I still didn't want to have that conversation. Back at the castle, pre-Cal, I'd always been a one-person kind of woman. The idea of multiple partners at once was unheard of, and the ladies at court would have given me a piece of my mind if they knew about it.

The drakes didn't have the same thought process as humans did. Several of the females on occasion even competed to see who was rutting with the most males, as if it were some kind of sport. It had caused Aryn to turn beat red for sure. My handmaiden was never one for loose tongues about intimate things. And the drakes were very loose with those togues of their's.

A hand waved in my face, jerking me from my thoughts.

Refocusing on Aryn, I noticed the deep turned-down frown on her face.

"What's wrong?" she signed. Did something happen?"

I shook my head, forcing a smile as I signed back. "What makes you think that?"

Aryn pointed at my hand.

I followed her gaze to see I had turned the edge of my skirt into a crumpled mess. Abruptly releasing it, I smoothed the wrinkles out with rapt attention. My ruse was not enough to sway Aryn. She knew well enough to be patient and wait for me to reveal myself.

Sighing, I glanced around the room. I didn't want the few female drakes who had begun to learn the language to see what I signed. Seeing the coast mostly clear, I answered Aryn.

"I'm just worried I might have messed things up."

Aryn arched her brow. "How so?"

Chewing on my bottom lip, I contemplated how to explain to Aryn that I'd not only given myself to one drake, but two. She'd be appalled for sure. Aryn already didn't like this situation, though she had begun to get along with many of the drakes during our stay here.

My hands moved to sign to her the mess I'd gotten myself into.

But before I barely got the words, "I did something stupid," out, a dark shadow formed over me.

Lifting my head, my eyes trailed over the large golden feet, up the stone and metal spiked plates on his knees and calves, I skipped over the middle bit, already feeling like this was going to end badly. Then I skimmed up the large chest covered in leather and bone before settling on the irate face of the drake king.

Swallowing a hard lump that had formed in my throat, I blinked up at the king with feigned innocence, waiting for him to address me.

"Your Highness, I require an audience with you, if it so pleases you," Ryu said aloud, his leips moving slow enough for me to follow. I couldn't hear the sarcasm in his voice, but the words were clear enough for me to see that this was not a random request for a quick romp.

The female drakes weren't even trying to act like they weren't interested in what was going on with Ryu. They all watched our interaction with increasing interest, Daylea's lips quirked up at the edge with a smugness I wanted to slap off her face.

Since Ryu hadn't offered me his hand like a gentleman, I pushed myself up to my knees and then climbed to my feet, brushing my hands off as I did so.

Aryn grabbed my hand.

I glanced at her, the worry in her expression squeezing my heart like a fist. I gave her a reassuring smile and patted her hand before pulling away.

Ryu walked in front of me, making no effort to act as if this was a pleasant interaction and I was nothing but a guest in their home. The two guards at the entrance of the female's quarter barely glanced our way as he passed by. I waited until we were out of range before pushing my thoughts at Ryu.

Where are we going?

No answer.

My brow furrowed. *Are you upset with me?*

Still no answer.

What in the gods was his problem? Was this to be my punishment? Keeping me in silence? Because I was used to it. I lived three years without speaking to others outside of signing and lip reading, I could do it again. I didn't need the voice in my head to survive. I truly didn't.

At first, I thought we would go back to his bedroom, but when the pathway started to decline, I knew we weren't headed anywhere good. I worried my lower lip wondering if I should just make a run for it.

If you run, I will chase you, and you won't like the outcome this time, princess.

My eyes widened at the growling in my head, removing any doubt that he hadn't heard me. The bastard was only trying to keep me off-balance while he took me to whatever punishment he had in mind for me.

Why should I punish you? Ryu's voice filtered into my mind with a hard tone as if he already knew the answer to the question.

Feigning innocence once more, I shrugged. *How am I supposed to know what you monsters like? Maybe this is some kind of monster mating ritual.*

Ryu jerked to a stop, and I bounced off his back. His tail tangled around my feet and knocked me to the ground. Rubbing my hip, I glared up at the drake king.

After all this time you still consider us monsters, princess?

Refusing to back down, I pushed to my feet and shoved a finger at his chest. *If you are going to act like monsters, then I can hardly think you are anything else. You are treating me as if I'm not your equal, and that in itself is a monstrosity. I am every bit as important as you.*

Ryu stared at me for a long moment. Finally, he opened his mouth, leaned his head back, and laughed. For a solid minute, the drake king laughed at me until my fingers curled into fists at my side. Unable to take it anymore, I reared back one of those fists and smacked him in the chest.

My hand throbbed, the fingers going slightly numb from the impact. I held the injured hand to my chest as tears burned my eyes, more from frustration than the pain in my hand. Ryu stopped laughing, concern flashing through his eyes before that cold wall went back in place.

You say you want to be treated as an equal, but were you treating me as such when you rutted with my brother and then avoided me for three days?

I sucked in a breath of pain. But not so much from my hurt hand, but because he was right. I hadn't been acting like he was my equal at all. Like what we had didn't matter.

However...

Staring down at my sore hand, I sniffed. "I apologize," I said aloud, while I explained more in my head. *I haven't been in this situation before — not that it's an excuse.* I lifted my gaze to the king's with a determined frown. *I don't know what this is —* I gestured between us. *— but I wasn't trying to hide what I did.* I blew out a breath. *I just didn't know how to explain it, since I wasn't sure if there was anything to explain.* I dropped my eyes down to the ground.

A clawed finger lifted my chin to meet his gaze. *I am not angry at you for rutting with my brother.*

You're not? I cocked a brow and then scowled. *Then what's all this about?* I gestured between us with my good hand.

The hand on my chin dropped down to wrap around my throat. Ryu lifted me, pushing me up against the wall of the corridor, until his face was inches from mine.

I might share with my brother on occasion but that still doesn't mean I won't punish you for going behind my back and avoiding me.

A cold shiver went down my spine at the threat while heat pooled between my thighs at what kind of punishment could be in store for me.

Chapter 21

RYU DRAGGED ME off the wall and down into a dark part of the mountain. My breath puffed out into the air in front of me. I'd have wrapped my arms around myself for warmth if Ryu didn't have my arm in a death grip.

Finally, he stopped us in front of a dark room. Ryu released me to walk over to what I guessed was the wall. Ryu's chest burned orange and red before fire burst from his mouth, making me flinch back.

Once my eyes adjusted and took in the metal chains on the wall, my feet stumbled back. Heart in my throat, I glanced at Ryu and then back at the chains before making a break for the entrance.

I didn't have a chance.

Ryu's hand wrapped around the back of my neck, jerking me back into the room. I kicked my feet, twisting around as I tried to get out of his grip.

Let me go. You're not going to chain me up here like some kind of criminal.

Turning me around, Ryu pushed me toward the wall, acting as if my scratching and kicking wasn't affecting him at all. I grunted and cried out, trying, and failing to get my arms out of his grip while Ryu chained one arm and then the other up above my head until my arms were taut. I still kicked out with my legs.

What the fuck is wrong with you? How is this a fair punishment?

Ryu caught one of my legs, drawing his hand down my exposed thigh until he reached my ankle. That would have been exciting had he not then clamped a metal cuff on it, leaving that leg chained to the wall. He cuffed my other leg before standing up, leaving me chained and helpless against the wall.

My chest heaved as I tried to keep my breathing even. The situation was too close to how Cal and Luis used to hold me down while the other cut into my skin, laughing and rubbing their erections along the marks they made.

Ryu grasped my throat and smoothed his fingers up and down the sides.

Breathe, princess. Breathe.

I shook my head rapidly. *I can't. I... This...*

Look at me, Ryu commanded in my head. I didn't, so he shook me slightly. *Look. At. Me.*

Slowly, I lifted my eyes to meet the chartreuse colored eyes of the drake king.

You are safe with me. Ryu's eyes stayed on mine, his fingers stroking my skin. *Do you believe me?*

While being chained to the wall made me feel helpless in the same way I had with Callahan, I truly didn't believe the drake would hurt me. He had ample time to do so, many chances to use my position for his own twisted sick pleasure, and yet he hadn't. Ryu wouldn't even touch me the first night until I touched him first.

This was punishment for avoiding Ryu rather than coming to him about Ira and me. If he was going to do something to me, I trusted that it wasn't going to be something cruel and hurtful. At least, not unless I was screaming for more by the end.

Swallowing, I inclined my head.

Lips curling up, Ryu stroked the side of my face. *Stay still.*

Ryu released my face and, quicker than I could gasp, he sliced through the straps of my top. It fell to the ground, leaving my breasts to hang free. If I thought the drake king would stop there, I would be wrong. My skirt soon followed my top, leaving me bare and shivering against the dirt and stone wall.

Taking a moment, Ryu's chartreuse eyes roamed over my form. He didn't skip any part of me. Not my breasts, my nipples pulled taunt by the cold. Not the scars crisscrossing along my stomach and sides. Then they found the branding on my side. The one scar I wished more than anything to scour from my body. Ryu's eyes darkened, and smoke and sparks puffed from his nose.

When Ryu's claw reached out to stroke along the lines of Cal's name, I couldn't help but flinch back.

I could remove it for you.

My eyes jerked up to his face. *What do you mean?*

Ryu opened his mouth as fire built up inside of the back of his throat. Realizing he intended to burn away the marks, I shook my head vigorously.

"No, no. I can't."

Closing his mouth, Ryu swallowed down the fire, making his chest and belly burn. One of these days, I would have to ask him how that worked. Today was not that day.

Licking my lips, I turned my face away, unable to bear the weight of his gaze.

After a long moment, Ryu moved in closer to me. I braced myself for what my punishment would be. My heart raced in my chest, my pulse pounded in my ears. His fingers brushed along the curve of my breasts, his claw scraping against my nipple before pulling at it between his two claws.

I sucked in a breath against the pinch. It didn't hurt, not really. It was more of a stinging sensation that shot down to my core, turning my fear and anxiety into liquid desire.

Ryu did the same to the other breast until both nipples were squeezed tight in his grasp. My head fell back, and I groaned, my back arching toward him. I shouldn't be letting him know I like this. Didn't it dismiss the point of being punished if I was enjoying it?

I couldn't bring myself to care as Ryu released one nipple and replaced his claws with his mouth. That hot cavern enveloped my nipple, his long tongue wrapping around the tip and pulling it between his teeth. His fangs scraped against it, causing my knees to nearly buckle. For that moment, I was thankful for the manacles holding me up.

A pressure built between my thighs, my insides clenching and unclenching with a need to be filled. I bucked my hips, hoping to relay my needs to the drake king.

If Ryu noticed, he ignored me. He laved at my nipple, pulling and sucking it until it was just this side of too much. Then Ryu let go, returning the blood flow to the piece of flesh. I cried out at the lack of friction, but then I thought he'd give the other breast the same attention. He surprised me when he lowered to his knees before me.

Ryu said he was going to punish me. However, if this was

what their punishments were like, I would take them any day all day.

Ryu loosened the chain on one of my legs and lifted it up and over his shoulder. I barely had a moment to register the motion before Ryu buried his face in between my legs. He inhaled my scent so deeply that if I hadn't been so aroused, I'd have been embarrassed. I almost held my breath waiting for that first lick against my throbbing clit. The anticipation was almost more than I could bear.

Ryu shifted his attention to the marks on my inner thigh instead, making me groan out in frustration. His fingers trailed over the mark Ira had left on my inner thigh and then the one he'd given me. Each touch sent zings of pleasure straight to my core, and I bucked against his face.

Instead of giving into my demands, Ryu took his time licking the mark he'd left, tracing along each part of the bite until he was almost to my pussy... But then, he skipped over it to give the same attention to my other thigh.

When he scraped his fangs along the vein there, I steeled myself. Was he going to mark me there too? Wasn't one enough?

Thankfully, he moved away from my thigh without biting me again. My hips jumped at the first lick of his tongue. The long split tip of it swirled and dipped into every crevice of my folds before circling around my clit.

I used the leg hooked over his shoulder to pull him closer to me, trying to get him to give me more, more, more.

Despite my urgings, Ryu took his time. His tongue moved across and through my folds as if he was trying to map it in his head, but never staying in one spot long enough for me to get to the edge. Ryu kept me on that edge until I fought against the restraints, pulling and tugging, rotating my hips to try and get him to stay where I wanted him to stay.

Minutes later, I was crying. My pussy raw and aching with unleashed need.

I was wrong. Wrong about everything.

The drake king was an evil cruel bastard.

Ryu stood, finally giving my folds a reprieve. My body revolted in a mixture of relief and protest.

Moving in close, Ryu grabbed me by the chin and licked his lips, letting his long tongue flitter across my own before tipping my head back and delving into my mouth, forcing me to taste myself on his tongue. That tongue then shoved further into my mouth and down my throat. Fighting against my gag reflex, I swallowed his tongue down, breathing through my nose until he finally released me.

Now, pet. Ryu brushed his fingers along the side of my face before cupping my chin in his hand. *Have you learned your lesson, or should we keep going?*

I shook my head, barely moving it in his grip. *No. Please no.*

My body ached, tensed, and coiled like a snake ready to strike but never would. I needed to come. I'd agree to practically anything to get the drake king to let me get over that precipice.

That's a good girl, Ryu purred in my mind. Then he pinched my clit.

The orgasm was so violent and sudden, my head threw back against the wall, my scream burned and scratched my throat, my hips bucking wildly until I was panting and crying into a slobbering mess.

While I sagged against the bonds, I was barely able to keep my eyes open. I knew one thing for certain. I'd never avoid Ryu ever again.

When I woke up a bit later, I was no longer in the dark dungeon but back in the drake king's bedroom.

Shifting on the bed, I winced and grimaced at the aches in my body. My clit throbbed with each move of my legs. Ryu's punishment definitely had lasting effects on me. Speaking of which...

Rolling over, I reached for Ryu on his side of the bed. My hand found an empty space and no drake king.

My lips turned down in a frown. Where did he go?

Sitting up, I threw my legs over the bed and stood. Immediately, the cool air hit my naked flesh, and I remembered Ryu had cut my clothing off. I grabbed the blanket and wrapped it around myself. Thankfully, Ryu had left the torches lit when he left.

Stepping out of the room, my eyes found Tat waiting in the corridor. My face heated for a moment.

Tat kept his eyes on my face, not once dropping below my neck. "Where to?" he signed, his hands slow and unsure.

I lifted my chin and used my arm to hold the blanket so I could sign a reply.

"Female's quarters."

We walked down the corridor without speaking to one another. I think Tat didn't know what to say or maybe he didn't want to say anything inappropriate. He certainly didn't want to accidentally look at me below the neck.

While Tat had the good sense to ignore the fact that I was wearing nothing but a blanket, the guards at the female's quarters did not. The blue one leered at me while the obsidian scaled one sneered with disgust.

Ignoring their looks, I left Tat at the door while I shoved into the room. A few of the drake females glanced my way, but no one really cared about what I was wearing. That wouldn't have been back at my castle. I could just imagine what the ladies of the court would have said if I walked in with only a blanket pulled around me.

Aryn sat between several drake females who were showing her how to weave a basket. At my appearance, her eyes widened, and she rushed to my side.

I waved her off. "I'm fine," I signed one-handed.

Beautine smirked from her seat.

I rolled my eyes. "Yes, I'm hilarious," I said. "Can I have something else to wear?"

Beautine said something to another female drake, who scuffled away. She returned a few moments later with a bundle of black cloth. I still had the material I'd gotten at the market. Unfortunately, I hadn't had time to figure out how to get it tailored. I might be skilled in many things, but a seamstress I was not.

Taking the clothing, I walked to the back area to change. This was a one-piece dress that clipped at the shoulders and trailed separately across my breasts before hooking in the middle below my breastbone. The rest of the cloth flowed into a skirt that had a slit up both sides. An intricate metal and leather belt held the whole thing together.

Sighing, I held my head high as I walked out of the female's quarters. Tat waited for me on the other side. He had the good sense not to ask any questions and simply let me lead the way.

Chapter 22

SITTING OUTSIDE AT the edge of the spring, my feet dangled in the water as I leaned back on my hands. I could almost pretend I was on some kind of holiday rather than trying to save my kingdom. The sun was warm on my face, and there were no clouds in the sky as if the gods themselves had wanted to give me a moment of peace.

I truly needed it.

After everything I'd given for my kingdom, I was a bit overwhelmed. I'd give my own life for the people of Kinoko, I would have, if Callahan had gotten his way. Now, here I was giving my body to not one drake but two!

My hands clutched the sides of my face as it heated. What would the ladies back at court think of me entertaining two males at once, and not even fully human ones at that.

I burst out laughing.

They wouldn't know what to think because the ladies at court were too prim and proper to do anything out of the ordinary. If they took lovers, it was discreetly. Gods forbid that anyone finds out they actually enjoyed the finer part of sex.

That was probably one of the reasons I had never quite gotten along with them, even before I lost my hearing. They would certainly cast me out of their little social circle for this. Or at least, they'd talk behind my back about it. Not that they didn't already do that now.

I huffed out a breath of air.

Twisting my body so I could see behind me, I searched for where my guard, Tat, waited at the tree line. The drake had agreed to escort me outside and since the drake king knew I wasn't going to run now that we were on the same side, I could come and go as I pleased. Still, I had to be careful. Callahan's men were swarming the woods still trying to find me.

I wasn't sure what the plan was. I'd done my part in getting the drakes to agree to help me. Now, it was up to them. They were the battle experts, not some pampered broken princess.

While Beautine had done her best to teach me to fight — I definitely felt stronger — I wasn't sure I would do well in a battle. How could I fight if I couldn't hear someone coming up on me? I would imagine in the heat of the battle there would be too many bodies and vibrations for me to use my usual way of finding those around me.

However, one on one? I think I could hold my own, at least until Ryu came to rescue me.

I giggled to myself.

Who would have thought a few weeks ago that I was curious but terrified of the drakes like a bedtime story monster? Now, I was hoping they would rescue me if I were in danger.

Leaning forward, I drew my legs out of the water and wrapped my arms around them as I leaned my chin on my knees. I just wished I knew what I was doing. I was tired of waiting. Tired of the ever-present worry gnawing at my stomach until I was sick with fear.

I wanted it to be like it was before my mother died. When I was carefree and innocent, not constantly thinking about being damaged goods or having to deal with sadistic princes. I would just dance and play with my mother while the world went by.

My eyes burned, and I shoved back the tears. There was no use crying over it. She was dead, and those days were long gone. This was my reality, and I had to suck it up and learn to deal with it.

After all, I wasn't some simpering princess stuck in a castle. I'd escaped the castle and gotten the help of the drakes. There was nothing I couldn't do.

Tired of feeling sorry for myself. I shoved myself up off the ground and onto my feet. Hands on my hips, I jerked my head in a nod. It was past time I learned what the battle plan was. Maybe I wasn't a master of battle like the drakes, but I was still an integral part of this whole operation. Without me, there would be no reason to fight.

Nodding my head once more, I pivoted on my heel, planning to head back inside and demand the drake king and his brothers to let me in on the planning. I would not sit idly by while they died for me. I needed to be a part of this.

"Come on, Tat. Time to go," I called out as well as signing, knowing the drake wanted to learn by doing as much as possible. But when my guide and now friend didn't appear by my side, I frowned. Where had he gone? I stomped forward towards where I had seen him last.

"Tat, come on!" I called out without bothering with my hands this time. "I'm ready to go back inside. I don't want to be the reason you get in trouble." Or me, I added silently.

A shiver ran down my back as I recalled the last time I'd gotten in trouble. Maybe I did want to be punished. Liquid gushed between my thighs, and I clenched them together tightly. This was not the time to be aroused. What would Tat think when he smelled it on me?

Of course, the drake had been a perfect gentleman. Never once had he tried to take any liberties with me, even before Ryu had marked me for all to know I belonged to him. Not that it would stop a human who didn't have their superior sense of smell, and I didn't plan on letting anyone see the new scar on my inner thigh any time soon.

Pushing that thought aside, I stalked further up the pathway back to the cave entrance. Maybe he'd decided to wait at the door?

My foot landed in something wet and warm. My face scrunched up in disgust, worried it was a bug or something, I lifted my foot to see dark red. My brows furrowed, I swiped a finger over it and lifted it to my nose. The coppery scent made my eyes widen and my heart race.

Blood.

Suddenly, I was on full alert. Spinning around in a circle, I looked for the source of the blood. For my guard, my friend. Not seeing him immediately or any origin of the spilled blood, I glanced back down at the ground. The blood led further into the woods. I stepped forward then stopped.

Chewing on the inside of my cheek, I debated what to do. If Ryu or Ira were here, they would both tell me to go back inside and find help. However, it might be too late by then. Tat could be seriously hurt.

I couldn't take that chance. After all, I'd learned to fight hand to hand against drakes. If humans had caused this, they should be nothing, right?

Making a decision, I curled my hands into fists and stepped into the woods. Eyes darting between the woods and the trail of blood which had only gotten thicker as I went, I searched for my friend. When the splotches of blood only grew in size, my feet quickened. This much blood loss wasn't good. I had to find him.

My foot hit something, and I fell forward, my hands catching me on the ground and scraping my palms. I winced and glanced back at what I'd tripped over.

Tat!

Scurrying around to his side, I checked to see if he was breathing. When I felt his hot breath on my hand, my shoulders relaxed. Still alive. Thank the gods.

I ran my hands over him until I found his wound. Several stab wounds covered his back, and when I turned him over, I found his front was just as bad. I pulled my lower lip between my teeth. Who could have done this? These weren't animal marks, this came from a blade.

Knowing I wasn't strong enough to drag the large drake back to the entrance on my own, I grabbed the dagger strapped to Tat's leg and cut at the bottom of my skirt. I wrapped his wounds the best I could, leaving my skirt just above my knees now from all the fabric I'd lost.

It would have to do for now. At least until I could get back to the lair and find someone to help him.

As I moved to stand, the sensation of cold steel against the skin of my throat made me freeze. Not moving my head, I glanced to the side, trying to see my attacker. I couldn't see much, just a dirty human hand and a coat sleeve the color of sand.

Callahan's colors.

Fuck. This wasn't good.

A movement out of the corner of my eye turned my attention to where five other soldiers all wearing Callahan's color and sigil stepped out of the tree lining. All of a sudden, my attacker jerked my head back by my hair until I stared at the menacing face of a man I didn't know.

I grunted but didn't demand he let go of me. They didn't want to talk, and if they didn't know who I was, I had a better chance of getting away from them. Hopefully unharmed. Tat didn't have much time, and I couldn't waste it with these idiots.

The man's mouth moved, and I made out the words. "Talk. Bitch."

Classy.

Refusing to give into his demands, I stared hard at him.

His gaze flicked up for a moment to the others nearby before his mouth moved again. This time I caught it.

"This is her?"

Shit.

My unresponsiveness had done the opposite of what I wanted. Well, if the jig was up, there was no point in being quiet about it.

"Let me go," I snarled at the man, while my fingers searched the for the blade I'd used to cut my skirt. If I could just reach it.

"Ah, so she can talk." The soldier sneered at me, then jerked my head back even more just as I tried to stretch my arm to grab the hilt of the dagger just out of my reach. "His Highness will give us a big reward for returning you to him. He's been missing his plaything so very much."

I snarled at his words. "I'm not a plaything. I'm a person. And His Highness can fuck off and die for all I care."

The metal against my neck traced along my jawline as he turned me more toward him.

"Maybe I'll punish you for him and blame it on the drakes," he sneered. "No one would believe you. Not after spending so much time with those monsters."

Someone on the other side must have said something because the man's brows furrowed, and his face scrunched up in anger and annoyance. His mouth formed one word.

"Fine."

He let me go with a shove, and before I could break my fall, a sharp pain hit the back of my head and everything went black.

Chapter 23
Desmond

"CAN WE JUST give her back?" Desmond pointed out, leaning over the map of the five kingdoms.

Ryu and Ira snarled at him with such vengeance that Desmond worried they would bite his head off just for mentioning it.

This wasn't going according to plan. Ryu was far too attached to the human princess and now surprisingly, Ira was too. Desmond was determined not to be caught up in her web, even if he teased her with it.

"Just hear me out, if we give her back," Desmond pushed forward with his hands up to pacify his brothers, "we can move somewhere else. Then there's no threat to any of our people."

"We're not giving her back," Ryu growled out, smoke trickling out of his mouth with the force of his rage.

"Come on, her pussy can't be that great." Desmond shook his head with a disgusted scowl, his tail whacking the floor with his irritation. "There are plenty of drake females who would love if you marked them. Why can't you just pick one of them?" Desmond scratched his chin with his claws. "Or maybe it's the human aspect? If that's the case, we can find you a new one."

Desmond barely dodged the swipe of Ryu's claws. Ira was right there at his back, his ire just as strong but his reaction more reserved. Ira had always been more in control of his emotions out of the three of them. Though when he finally did burst, it burned with such a ferocity that the whole world would tremble.

"Just because there's no female who wants to become attached to you doesn't mean you have to shit all over ours." Ryu grabbed Desmond by the horns and shoved his forehead against his brother. "Don't talk about things you do not understand."

Desmond pushed his brother back with his head, growling and baring his teeth at him. "What I understand is that you think some pussy is worth all our lives when we can just leave."

With a roar, Ryu threw Desmond away from him.

Desmond's back hit the stone and dirt wall with a crack. Wincing, he leaned against the wall until his vision stopped spotting.

"Tell me, brother," Ryu spat, his body wavering in his vision. "Are you going to tell our people that we have to leave? That they must pick up everything they have built over the last five decades and start all over again? Because I won't do it."

"Coward," Desmond coughed out, dragging in a breath as he pushed himself back to standing with his tail.

"No, you are the coward for wanting to run when we should stand and fight."

Desmond glared at his brother and king, not wanting to admit he was right. Drakes didn't run, they stood their ground and razed anything that got in their way to the ground. This was different, though. Whenever a female was involved, it always was.

"She doesn't belong to you," Desmond reminded Ryu and then shot a look at Ira. "Either of you. She's already spoken for. Marking her doesn't make her yours."

"That's not how it happened, and you know it. She came to us. That prince of hers," Ryu spat with a flash of his fangs, "doesn't deserve her. He will only end up killing her and then us, if he has his way."

"Then we make a deal," Desmond tried again. "We contact

this prince and tell him we'd trade the princess back for a treaty with them so they won't attack us."

Ira chuckled. "When have humans ever kept their word?"

"We could at least try," Desmond snapped, stepping forward. "Better than just going along with whatever some princess wants. All we have is her word for it. How do we know she's not lying?"

Ira shook his head with a sad frown. "You haven't seen the scars, Des. You don't know what he's done to her."

"So? You told me about the scars. So what? We all have scars." He threw a hand at Ira's face. "What makes this any different?"

Ira's face hardened. "Hearing about them and seeing them are two different things. This isn't some scar she got on the battlefield. This bastard tortured her for his own amusement. Carved his very name into her flesh so she wouldn't forget she belonged to him."

Desmond swallowed the bile that threatened to rise in him.

"Tell me." Ira lifted his chin and stared down at Desmond. "Would a female drake let that kind of thing stand?"

"No," Desmond said softly as he shook his head. "They'd scoop their guts out with their claws before it ever got that far."

"Exactly."

Ryu gripped Desmond's shoulder with a sigh. "She may be human, but she has the heart of a dragon. We would be fools to run away from this."

Desmond huffed a breath and nodded, knowing he wasn't going to win this one. Maybe if he talked to Georgia, he could get her to see reason or find some way that their people were caught in the crossfires.

"Very well." Desmond offered a weak smile to both his brothers. "Where is our fearless princess anyway?"

Ryu shrugged. "At the clearing with Tatoween, I think."

"Alone?" Desmond arched a brow. "Is that wise?"

Ira snorted. "She's not going to run away."

"I mean if that prince of hers is looking for her, she shouldn't be out there alone even with a guard."

Ryu patted Desmond's shoulder. "I think one drake can take on a few humans. We've done so before."

A sinking cold feeling crept into Desmond's belly. He didn't like this, not at all. Not after the recent run in with the humans.

Spinning on his heel, Desmond stalked down the corridors toward the exit that led to the clearing. For a moment, he thought his brothers weren't going to come, but a few moments later, the resounding thud of their steps as they rushed to catch up with him filled his ears.

"You really think something is wrong?" Ira asked, coming up beside him.

Desmond shook his head. "I don't know. I just have this feeling.

Either way, it doesn't hurt to check on her, right?"

Ryu frowned and then chuckled warily. "So worried for her safety now, are you?"

"If she's the only thing standing between us and annihilation then fuck yes, I am," Desmond snapped as they grew close to the entrance. He paused his nose lifting to sniff the air.

"Blood," he announced before his footsteps quickened.

They burst out of the cave entrance, the bright sun stinging Desmond's eyes for a moment before pushing forward. Ryu rushed toward the edge of the spring where Georgia's shoes sat while Ira stopped halfway down the path.

"She was here." Ryu held up her shoes. "But why would she leave her shoes behind?"

"Maybe she forgot them," Desmond answered, hoping speaking the words would make them true.

"And the blood?" Ira asked, kneeling one knee on the ground, his fingers touching the drying red substance. He lifted it to his nose and sniffed. "It's drake blood."

So the princess was okay. The tension in Desmond's tail relaxed before he realized what that meant.

"Does that mean...?" Desmond trailed off as Ira moved into the woods. Desmond glanced at Ryu before chasing after Ira, following the scent of blood as it got thicker.

The sight of the drake on the ground made Desmond's heart stutter. He didn't particularly care for Tatoween one way or the other, but no one should be left to die bleeding out alone.

"That's material from Georgia's clothes," Ira stated from where he knelt beside the drake. He touched the cloth wrapped around the multitude of stab wounds already bleeding through the fabric. Desmond watched as Ira tested the drake for breath and then placed his ear against his back.

"He's breathing but barely. His heart is weak. Georgia binding his wounds is the only reason he hasn't bled out already. But we need to get him to the infirmary quickly."

"Obviously they were attacked, but where's Georgia?" Ryu said from behind him, his nose to the air. "I can smell her scent, but it's fading. It's been an hour at least."

He walked around the clearing, sniffing as he went.

"Are you listening to me?" Ira asked Ryu. "He's going to die if we don't get him back."

"Then take him," Ryu snarled, his eyes flashing and his claws flexing by his sides. "I'm going to find our princess."

"Maybe she finally ran away?" Desmond offered up, trying not to sound too hopeful.

Ryu shook his head. "No, the ground is disturbed with multiple footprints, and they go this way the same direction her scent went. Someone attacked them and grabbed Georgia."

Desmond stepped up to his brother, avoiding his swinging tail as he glared out at the woods.

"We'll get her back, Ryu. But we have to get Tatoween to the infirmary first. We can't go rushing after her with no plan or idea of where she was taken."

Snarling a huff, Ryu turned to him. "You're right. I just hope they didn't take her back to that bastard yet. If he touches one hair on her head, it'll be the last thing he ever does."

Chapter 24

I COULDN'T TELL what woke me. One minute I was dreaming about a delicious set of drakes and then the next my eyes were blinking open.

Wincing at the sudden light, I quickly shut my eyes again. Why was it so bright? The torches in Ryu's room never burned my eyes like this.

I shifted, and rolled onto my back, reaching across the bed for Ryu. My hand didn't meet scales or the fur blanket that was usually beneath me. My fingers slid across the surface of the... ground? How did I get on the ground?

I forced my eyes to open. Squinting through the brightness until my eyes adjusted, I turned my head to one side and then the other. The walls were made of fabric, a dark blue lined with gold. There was a flap that fluttered in the wind giving me glimpses of the outside.

A tent?

Frowning at the reason I would be inside a tent made me sit up and rub the back of my head where it ached. My hand paused and my eyes widened.

That's right, some of Callahan's guards knocked me out after trying to help Tat. My heart raced at the thought of my drake friend still lying there in the woods, bleeding out. How could this have happened?

I should have just stayed inside. I knew there were guards searching for me and still I had to insist that I get some air. Guilt ravaged me, and I grabbed at my chest.

Would someone find him before it was too late? Did they know I was missing? What would Ryu do once he found out I was gone? What about Aryn?

I had too many questions and no way to answer them. I just needed to calm down. Think this through.

Someone would come searching for me before too long, and then they would find the trail of blood just like I did. Hopefully, they found Tat before it was too late and then they will realize I'm missing.

Ryu and his brothers are smart. They would figure out that I didn't run away, but had been taken. They wouldn't blame Aryn for this. They might even ask for her help in finding me. Or would they?

Ryu had agreed to help me fight Callahan, but now that I was back in his hands, I didn't know if the drake king would actually come for me. Would they consider it too much of a risk? Or would they continue on without me?

I wasn't vital in their planning to fight against Callahan. In the long run, it didn't matter if I lived or died. Really, I was just an unnecessary distraction. A liability.

No. I couldn't rely on them to come save me. There was no telling what the drakes would do. I had to figure a way out of this on my own.

Pushing myself to my knees, I tried to stand and fell back on my butt. The world spun around me, and my stomach rolled. Taking slow shallow breaths, I inched my way back up to my knees, grabbing onto the desk nearby for support.

My eyes fell on the desk. Papers were strewn across the dark wood top along with a small dagger on the corner. A few of them caught my eye. A map of the five kingdoms. One of Kinoko and of... Plumus? Why would they need a map of their own kingdom?

Movement out of the corner of my eye had me curling my fingers around the dagger. I drew my arm down to my side, concealing the blade as I glared up at my least favorite person.

Callahan.

"Ah, she awakens." Callahan smiled at me as if he were seeing me on a social call rather than having his soldiers grab me and almost kill my friend.

Eyes narrowed, I used the desk to lift myself up off the ground.

"Don't get up," Callahan continued as he walked toward me, this time using his hands as he spoke. "I think I like seeing you on your knees."

Ugh. Kill me now.

"So you can sign," I croaked out, not using my hands so as to keep the dagger hidden. "Guess that means you're just an asshole then, but then again... we already knew that."

Callahan's smile just widened. "I always liked that fire in you. I'm so glad your time with those monsters hasn't dampened it. I would hate to have a boring old wife."

"I'll never be your wife," I snarled, baring my teeth at him. I'd rather die. Then you can run back to your father like the failure you are."

His hand shot out and struck me, my face whipping to the side. My cheek stinging, I tasted the blood on the edge of my lip and smirked.

"I guess the honeymoon is over?" I taunted him, lifting my chin to look down my nose at him. It was a bit hard to do from the ground, but I managed.

Callahan grabbed me by the face. His fingers squeezed my cheeks together as he leaned over me.

"Oh, my love, the honeymoon is just getting started." He pressed his lips against mine, shoving his tongue into my mouth.

I grunted and struggled against his hold. Tempted to bite his tongue off, my fingers curled around the handle of the dagger instead. Almost smiling into the forced kiss, I shoved at him with one hand while slowly lifting the dagger.

All I had to do was stab him in just the right place and all this would be over. No war, no need to put anyone else at risk. If I could just kill the reason behind all my issues, we could all have our happily ever after.

A thought flickered in my mind that surprised me.

What about Ryu? What about Ira? If this all ended, did everything go back to the way it was before? The Kinokos pretending the drakes didn't exist and the drake hiding away in the mountain like a noble's secret bastard child.

When the snake's hand tried to pull up my skirt, he decided for me.

I flipped the dagger in my hand and shoved up. Callahan shoved me away before I could finish driving it home. I hit the ground hard, my teeth jarring in my head.

Before I could see the damage I had done, Callahan was on me.

With one hand, he grabbed my hair at my scalp, jerking my head back while his other grabbed my dagger hand. His grip tightened like a vise until I cried out and dropped the dagger. It fell to the ground where Callahan kicked it across the ground.

"Look who learned a few new tricks." Callahan wagged his finger at me with a cluck of his tongue. "Now, that wasn't very nice."

I spit in his face. "Now you know how it feels, *Cal*."

"Oh, sweet precious Georgia." He laughed and didn't bother to wipe my saliva off his face. "There is nothing you can do to me that my dear old father hasn't already done."

I sniffed. The idea of someone cutting up the asshole in front of me caused a bit of joy to spark in my heart.

"Boo hoo. Like father, like son, I suppose."

Callahan jerked me by the hair, making me hiss. "I'm nothing like him."

"Tell that to the scars on my body," I growled, kicking a leg out in a move that Beautine had taught me. My foot hit the front of his knee, and Callahan crumbled before me, releasing his grip on my hand and braid.

I scrambled away on all fours, before shoving up onto my feet and heading for the tent opening. I flipped the tent cover open and ran into a hard wall of muscle. Hands grabbed my arms, and my eyes jerked up to meet those of my second least favorite person.

Luis.

"Well, well." His eyes darkened, skimming over me before glancing behind me and into the tent. "Seems like I'm right on time. Need a hand, brother?"

Of course this would be just my luck.

Chapter 25
Ira

RYU WANTED TO go barreling into the Plumus prince's camp, laid out on the outskirts of the Gebe forest. How did the prince get permission to bring so many of his own men into the country? There was no way that the Kinoko's king would ever approve such a move. It was just asking the other kingdoms to attack.

"Brother, please," Desmond appealed to Ryu for the fifth time since they'd gathered on the edges of the forest. "She isn't worth it. Let's just go back, gather our people, and leave. Let them fight it out amongst themselves."

Ira could see Desmond's side of things. A strange female came into their lives only to thrust their entire race into danger. If Ira hadn't seen the scars on Georgia's pale luscious skin himself, he would have thought she was playing a game as well.

But the scars didn't lie and neither did Georgia. This prince wouldn't stop until he took the kingdom and destroyed them all.

Ryu snarled and grabbed Desmond by the throat, shoving him against the trunk of a nearby tree.

"Either you are going to help us, or you can go back to the mountain. I won't have you causing the rest of our people to be put in danger because you are hesitant to get involved."

"But brother —"

Smoke and a bit of flame puffed out of Ryu's nose. "Am I clear?"

Desmond's chest grew bright with his anger, smoke curling out of his nose and mouth.

"Crystal," he snarled.

Ryu released him with a shove. "Then let's move."

Ira moved from his place against the tree he'd been leaning on, his tail flicking from side to side. "If we are done discussing this, I still think one of us should scout out the area before attacking in mass."

"We don't have time," Ryu scowled, his head turning toward Ira. "We don't know what that bastard of a prince is doing to her right now. I won't have a single mark on her body."

"You have to have more confidence in Georgia." Ira uncrossed his arms and stepped closer to his brother, lowering his voice so the other drake soldiers didn't overhear their conversation. No need to worry about them when it wasn't needed. "Beautine has taught her well, and she will have the element of surprise on her side." Ira's lips ticked up at the thought of the look on her betrothed's face when the helpless broken princess finally bit back.

Ryu assessed Ira for a moment before nodding his agreement.

Desmond arched a brow at Ira, his voice trickling into his head.

Thank you.

Ira flashed a nasty grin at his brother. *I didn't do it for you.*

Desmond sighed and rubbed a hand between his horns. *This female is going to be the death of us. I just know it.*

Then you better get on board because she's not going anywhere, Ryu snapped into both of their minds with a definitive slap of his tail against the ground.

Ira snorted and patted Ryu on the shoulder. "Let's get her back first before we make life-altering statements. Besides, who's to say she's going to stick around after all this? Maybe we're just an adventure, something she grins and bares until she can get what she wants."

"Exactly what I've been trying to say all along." Desmond threw his hands up with a release of breath. "We help her, she turns on us, and then we are back where we started. Hiding out from the humans, short an unknown number of drakes because we helped her fight the Plumus." Ryu opened his mouth to argue but Desmond continued as if he hadn't noticed. "Who, as you know, hate us and anyone different."

"All the more reason to defeat them," Ira commented with a pointed look at them both. This was getting out of control, and knowing their brother, Desmond had a hundred and one reasons why he shouldn't get out of bed in the morning, let alone help a princess save her kingdom.

"Ira has a point." Ryu inclined his head in Ira's direction, his hand going to the hilt of his sword. "We're wasting time. We're going."

"Another point I was about to make." Desmond jumped in front of Ryu as he pulled his machete from his back. He spun it in his hands and pointed the sharp edge at Ryu's throat. "Where will we go?"

Ryu grabbed the metal point in his palm and jerked it away from his neck. "What do you mean?"

"Since you don't seem to want to run now, where are we going to run when the inevitable happens and we actually do have to run?" Desmond clicked his tongue and shook his head. "We can't go to Plumus. Like you said, they hate us."

Ryu snorted.

"Can't go to Caffew. They don't have anything for us to hide in. Nothing but endless plains, no mountains unless we want to dig a tunnel?" Desmond cocked a brow. "I didn't think so."

"You're being dramatic, brother," Ryu growled, shoving Desmond's weapon back at him. "Perhaps you should move into the female's quarters."

"Haha, very amusing." Desmond hooked his machete on his back and stared out in between the trees. "What I'm saying is that we aren't thinking this through. This is a big risk for very little reward, if any. I just don't see the point."

Ira shook his head, pushing off the tree he'd been leaning on. "Sometimes it's not about the reward. It's about doing what is right."

Desmond snorted. "Says our shadow master. Tell me, brother. Did you feel like you were doing right all the times you were torturing the soldiers for information?"

Narrowing his gaze on his younger brother, Ira pressed his lips tightly together until he could taste his blood as his fangs stabbed into his lips. "That is not the same and you know it."

"Regardless," Ryu stepped between the two of them, "we promised to help Georgia, and drakes always keep their word."

"You promised," Desmond pointed out, not ready to give up the argument yet. "I don't remember any of us agreeing with you." He waved a hand to the drake soldiers behind him. "Why don't you ask them if they want to risk their life for your human mistress?"

Ira watched the interaction, waiting for Ryu's patience to run out. If anyone knew how to push their older brother until he blew, it was Desmond. It was only a matter of time before Desmond pushed Ryu too far, and if Ira wasn't mistaken, that twitch beneath Ryu's eye was the lid about to be blown off.

Eyes on that twitch, Ira waited with bated breath for it to happen. Three...

"She's not that great. We have other females you could have."

Two...

"Besides, why would you want a princess? They're full of so much drama. Not to mention the nasty prince of hers to deal with."

One...

Ira snapped his fingers just as Ryu released a full mouthful of fire and smoke right at Desmond. The soldiers nearby flinched and stepped back from the conflagration. The trees behind Desmond smoldered and burned until it left a half a dozen or more trees on fire.

Ira cleared his throat. "Ryu."

He didn't answer or stop.

"Ryu," Ira tried once more. "If you are planning on this being a surprise attack, you might want to stop showing them our exact location."

Ryu's mouth clamped shut, cutting off the fire and smoke. Taking in a big breath, Ryu created a funnel, suctioning in all the fire and smoke he'd spit out until he swallowed it down. His chest burned bright with the amount of fire he took in, shining on the smirking face of their younger brother.

Desmond brushed some of the trees' ash off his shoulders. "Did that feel better?"

Ryu huffed and puffed before rubbing a hand over his face with a weary sigh.

"What am I going to do with you?"

Ira's eyes flicked to the tree line. "I would figure that out later. We have company."

Three soldiers in sand-colored uniforms stepped between the trees. They took one look at the drake brothers and their soldiers before turning on their heels and running the other way.

"Well?" Desmond cocked a brow. "Are we going to stop them or let them ruin our ambush? Come on, we have a princess to save."

Ira shook his head at his brother's mercurial nature before whipping his axe off his back. Time to save a princess indeed.

Chapter 26

I NEVER WANTED to be back in the clutches of Callahan or his brother. If I had the power, I would have chosen death first.

Coming face to face with my worst nightmare had my heart racing and my breath coming in rapid succession. Facing off against one of them was one thing, but being pinned between both of them with no way out had me close to fainting. Which would be worse because who knew what they would do to me then?

"You have been a naughty girl." Luis waved a finger at me with a malicious grin on his face.

My eyes darted from Luis to Callahan and back, unable to focus on just one of the threats.

Choosing to focus on the man in front of me instead of Callahan, I watched Luis's mouth move with increasing panic.

"I think she needs to be punished. Don't you, brother?" Luis stared over my head at Callahan. With my back to him, I didn't know what his response was, though I was sure it wasn't anything pleasant.

Luis still had his hands firmly gripping my arms, and he tried to push me back into the tent. I was so overwhelmed by both of them, I let myself step back.

Once.

Twice.

Then as if coming out of a haze, I stiffened my body and stopped.

What was I doing? I didn't have to do what they wanted anymore. They couldn't kill me. They needed me to steal the kingdom. I didn't need to roll over like a good little princess and take it anymore. Nothing, not even the safety of my kingdom, was worth giving myself over to them again.

When I stopped moving, Luis frowned.

Before Luis could question me, I grabbed his elbow and slammed my forehead into his face, aiming for the nose. Luis' hands flew to cover his face in pain, releasing me. I followed up with a kick to his knee, just like Beautine showed me, and he buckled.

Pushing him out of the way, I rushed past and made for the exit. If I could just get out of here, I could find a way back to the drakes or even my father. I could finally tell him what had been going on, and we could get rid of the Plumus bastards together.

But before I got two steps, a sharp yank at my head jerked me off my feet. I landed on my butt with a stinging impact.

Glaring up at Callahan, I tried to maneuver away from him, but his hold on my hair was too tight. I kicked out, hoping to hit him anywhere, preferably his cock.

Callahan laughed and dodged my attacks with ease. He shot a

look at his brother, his mouth moving at an angle I couldn't see.

Taking advantage of the distraction, I grabbed at the hand holding me, digging my nails into his flesh.

Callahan's attention moved back to me, and his lips curled on one side. "Oh, love, harder. That's just how I like it."

Gnashing my teeth at him, I jerked and twisted in his grip, grabbing for anything I could get my hands on to throw at him. Callahan laughed at me the whole time. For the first time ever, his face was full of pure joy instead of the fake happiness he radiated in front of my father and the court.

To my dismay, Luis found his footing and swiped his hand over his face, dragging blood across it from his broken nose. He took one look at me and stalked across the tent.

His slap hit me so hard I saw stars. My vision darkened at the edges, and I knew I was close to passing out. But I couldn't. Not near these two. Stay awake. Stay awake.

While my world spun, they moved my body around until I was sitting in a chair. As soon as Callahan released my hair, I tried to bolt. He grabbed hold of it once more, holding me there while Luis tied my hands and feet to the chair.

Once they seemed happy that I couldn't get out of my bonds, they turned to one, another speaking as if I wasn't even there.

"You okay?" Callahan touched his brother's nose.

When Luis winced, I smirked. Luis waved Callahan off and gestured at me.

"Where'd all that come from? That fight wasn't there before."

Callahan shot a grin at me before answering his brother. "Likely the drakes' bad influence. Don't worry, all she needs is a little training and then she'll be as docile as a flower."

Luis crossed his arms and his nose twitched, followed by another wince.

While they talked about me like I wasn't there, I really took a moment to look around me this time. The dagger laid on the ground where I'd dropped it. The papers on the desk were scattered over the side and covered the dirt floor.

But something tickled my nose, so I sniffed the air.

Burning wood? Were we in some kind of camp?

I already knew we were outside. First, we were in a tent, but second, I caught a glimpse at the sky around Luis before he shoved me back inside. What I didn't know was if we were alone.

I almost shook my hand and scoffed aloud. What was I thinking? These two primping princes wouldn't be caught dead out in the wild alone.

No, that means there are others. But how many? Was it just

Callahan's guards from earlier or was there more?

I needed to see outside the tent to assess my situation. and if I could get the information back to the drakes, all the better.

My mind drifted to my father wondering if he missed me or had even figured out what was going on.

Then as if thinking about him made him appear, my father brushed through the tent's opening. Immediately, I jerked at my bonds and tried to go to him but couldn't.

My father's eyes fell on me, and a frown marked his face. His mouth moved with his hands.

"Why is she tied up?"

Callahan and Luis exchanged a glance before turning their backs on me to talk to my father. I didn't want to give the bastards a chance to make up a story, so I raised my voice.

"Father, help me! They attacked me. They're not what they seem. They've been hurting me. I didn't let you know before because I didn't want you to worry, but now you have to see the monsters that they are."

I couldn't past Callahan and Luis to see what my father was saying. My helplessness threatened to swallow me. Tears burned my eyes as I pulled and tugged at the rope, never stopping my pleas for my father to help me.

Then Callahan's head turned to Luis, and he shrugged.

Luis pulled a dagger from his waist belt and grabbed my father by the shoulder, the dagger's sharp tip pressed to his throat. At the movement, I could see the look of terror and betrayal on my father's face. The wrinkles on his usually happy face were bunched up as they swiftly shifted to anger.

Based on previous experience, I knew the words out of his mouth were not quiet ones.

"What in the Underworld do you think you are doing? Unhand me this instant."

Luis didn't.

I waited for my father's guards to come running to his rescue. When no one came, my brows furrowed. Surely my father didn't come here alone. Where were his guards?

Callahan produced another chair, and Luis proceeded to lead my father to it at dagger point. Callahan looked at me then and started signing as he spoke.

"This is what's going to happen, princess. You're going to marry me, or I'll kill your precious father. Understood?"

I'd been wrong. There was something worse than being at their mercy, and Callahan had found it.

I looked at my father. His hands were bound now as well so he couldn't sign to me. His eyes and mouth beseeched me to say no.

That would be a selfish choice, the choice that would keep me out of the clutches of these two lunatics.

For how long, though?

If I didn't say yes, they would just find another way to make me do it. They had both of Kinoko's royals at their mercy and they could take over the kingdom all on their own.

"Why do you even want to marry me?" I sagged in my chair already knowing what my answer would be. "Kill both of us and you have our kingdom. We don't have to be married for that."

Callahan smiled and tipped my chin up with his fingers. "Ah, but I do. A kingdom overtaken by an enemy would revolt. Many would die on both sides. But our kingdoms united by marriage?" His thumb stroked the column of my throat. "Now that's something to celebrate. Too bad you'll be dead before our first anniversary."

So my choices were to let my father die or for both of us to die later.

If I was the praying type, I'd pray for the goddess to come save us. To have the drakes find us in the nick of time and make this all a bad dream. However, the goddess never brought my hearing or my mother back and she wouldn't save me now.

The choices weren't in my favor and I couldn't count on the drakes to come rushing in at just the right time. I had to make a plan. One that didn't end up with me or my father dead.

But what could I do? What could I offer Callahan to keep me and my father alive until the drakes rallied to fulfill their promise?

My stomach twisted into a sick knot as I realized exactly what Callahan wanted.

Then I had an idea.

I would give Callahan exactly what he wanted. Me as his wife. Then I'd turn his own plan against him and slit his throat while he slept. Perfect.

Staring up into Callahan's face, picturing all the ways I would murder him afterward, I grinned, I could feel that it wasn't a happy

one   but   one   that   promised
violence.

"Alright then. Have it your way.
Let's get married."

Chapter 27

OF ALL THE ways I imagined my wedding day, it was not this.

The priestess standing before me had a wary look on her face. Her dark eyes kept bouncing between Callahan and me. The stiffness in her shoulders showed how not okay with this arrangement she was.

I didn't blame her. Neither was I.

Callahan wanted me to marry him just so he could kill me later. However, he could at least give me a proper wedding.

I glared down at my torn and dirty outfit. My thoughts drifted to the dress sitting in my wardrobe. That dress had been my mother's before she died. My father gave it to me specifically for my wedding. My heart clenched tight as a fist as I thought of that dress never getting worn.

Though it was probably for the best. I wouldn't want to waste such a gorgeous gown on someone like Callahan. I'd rather see the dress burned to ash than for Callahan to leave one dirty paw on it later.

A lump lodged in my throat, making it hard to swallow.

The thought of what was going to happen after we were married terrified me. I was trying extremely hard not to think about it. Beautine had given me all these new tools to use to protect myself and yet those skills had meant absolutely nothing when it was all said and done.

Maybe if I'd been up against one of them, but both of them?

Impossible.

I had to be smarter about this. I'd bought mm and my father time by agreeing to marry Callahan. Now, I just had to get through this farce of a wedding until we got somewhere I wasn't surrounded by ten thousand soldiers.

The priestess couldn't seem to ignore them the way I had forced myself to do. She kept glancing at all the soldiers and weapons before shifting in place, her gold-lined white robe's movement giving away her anxiety.

Right there with you, lady.

My head turned slightly to where my father stood with Luis. To anyone else, it would seem like my father was happily watching his only daughter get married to a crazy maniac at knife point.

Callahan's hand on my elbow tightened.

I turned my wince into a smile which ended up being more a grimace, judging by the priestess's worried expression.

Callahan gestured a hand to the priestess to continue.

Startled by his abruptness, the priestess dapped her face with the sleeve of her robe. Her mouth moved so minutely that I couldn't understand a thing she was saying. Though, for the moment, I didn't need to know. It was a basic wedding ceremony. I'd been to many of the weddings for ladies of the court. I could practically recite the thing from memory.

"We come before our glorious goddess, Ainan'us, to unite these two souls. For this will be their final journey as individuals and will now journey through life as one."

Pause for ohs and ahs.

"For nothing is greater than the union of two souls under the most important emotion of all..." Pause for dramatic effect... "Love."

Ow, fuck.

I shot a glare at Callahan. He stared hard at me before jerking his head toward the priestess. I blinked at him before turning my attention back to the woman before me. Her mouth moved once more, and I still couldn't make out a word she was saying. Her lips moved fast, but in tiny movements.

Giving up trying to read her lips, I shook my head and shrugged.

Callahan rubbed a hand over his face and looked over at his brother. He spoke over my head, and his breath brushing my hair made me tense. The hand on my elbow tightened for a moment before he released me.

Immediately, I wanted to bolt. The need was so massive that I had to dig my still bare heels into the ground to keep myself from moving from that spot.

"She asked you to repeat after her," Callahan signed.

I arched my brow. Really? How was I supposed to do that?

Callahan seemed to figure out the issue and said a few words to the priestess before turning back to me. His hands moved as the priestess said a few words.

"Are you, name –" What the fuck, he couldn't even spell my name? Asshole.

"– of sound of mind and body and accept this man into your bed, your heart, and your soul? From now until the underworld takes you?"

I almost laughed and had to pretend to cough to cover it up. Was there an option for no to all the above? Callahan wasn't happy about my hesitation and grabbed my elbow once more. The pinch of his grip no doubt bruised me even more than I already was.

Still, I hesitated.

This wasn't something that I went into lightly, just like the decision to keep quiet about Callahan's and Luis's abuse of me before. I would bear this to save my king and kingdom. Just as I have done my whole life.

My gaze slid away from Callahan and the priestess to shift over to my father. He had never been very good at hiding his feelings. It had gotten him in trouble several times with other nobles. When he should have been cool and collected on the outside, he let his emotion hang all over his face and body posture.

Every muscle in his face screamed for me to say no. For me to stop all this and save myself. But what kind of daughter would I be if I let my father die because of me?

My father's hands lifted in front of him. They shook with every movement giving away the terror inside of him, even if his face was pushed into a forced smile. Before he could even sign one word to me, Luis grabbed my father's arm. His lips moved next to my father's ear, and suddenly my father's hands dropped, his face white as a specter.

"I do," I said aloud, a biting smile on my lips. "Until death. Though it may be sooner for one of us than the other."

The priestess's eyes widened, and her mouth dropped open. Her eyes darted from me to Callahan, likely wondering if I was joking. I wish I was.

The absolute hatred that burned in Callahan's eyes was nothing compared to the burn of

Ryu's fire. Callahan wanted to hit me, and I knew I would pay for that extra remark later.

The priestess's mouth moved again, and this time, Callahan didn't interpret for me, his eyes on the priestess the entire time. His jaw tight, his mouth barely moved as he answered the question the priestess posed to him.

The priestess approached me with a knife, and I stayed frozen still as she cut a long piece of my hair off. She then went to Callahan and did the same thing. Pressing the two pieces together, she wrapped them with a purple ribbon tying it into a bow before presenting it to us.

Callahan grabbed me around the waist and even though I knew it was coming, I couldn't prepare myself for the press of his lips against mine. It was funny how, after all the things Callahan had done to me, this was the one that disgusted me the most. This hard press of our lips together, the biting pressure of his teeth mashed against mine, this was what made me want to throw myself off the top of the castle tower.

I let him kiss me so the whole world could see that we were happily married before he finally released me. The ground rumbled as the soldiers stomped their feet and slammed their weapons on the ground and other places. Callahan gripped my elbow once more and waved to the soldiers. His mouth moved, but I didn't try to read what he was saying.

I was married. Married to a monster that wanted to kill me and my father, then enslave my whole kingdom. But before that, he would make my life as torturous and painful as possible.

The whole statement was so ridiculous, I could laugh. So I did. I burst out laughing until my stomach hurt and tears ran down my face.

Callahan looked at me like I'd lost my mind and perhaps I had.

Because only an insane person would marry someone they hated just for the chance to kill them later.

Chapter 28
Ryu

HIS BROTHERS AND ryu dragged the dead bodies of the Plumus soldiers into the woods. They couldn't have their presence noticed yet. There was much to learn before they could go barreling into the Plumus camp.

"Well?" Ryu asked Desmond who just came back from scouting the area. "What have you found out?"

Desmond didn't answer right away, his tail tense on the ground behind him. The two drakes he'd taken with him exchanged looks before taking a step back from them as if they didn't want to be in the line of fire.

Ryu scowled, his muscles bunched up with tension. "Don't hold back. We don't know how much time we have left. We need to get Georgia back."

Something on Desmond's face made Ryu think that his brother was holding his thoughts back. Even if Desmond wasn't a hundred percent in agreement with them about helping Georgia, Ryu could trust that he would do his job, no matter how disgruntled he was about it.

Desmond sighed and adjusted his weapon on his back. "You're not going to like it."

"I didn't ask whether or not I would like it. I want to know what you found out."

Every minute they wasted was another minute Georgia was with those sadistic assholes. Just the thought of them placing their hands on her made Ryu's chest burn. He wanted to find her. He needed to find her. Ryu could say that he needed to find her just for the drakes' sake. However, the fiery princess had found a way to wiggle her way under his scales and make herself at home.

"We couldn't get close enough to get a full account of the soldiers, but they weren't just a small group there to protect their prince." Desmond flicked his eyes over to Ira. "There had to be at least a few thousand or more. There's a lot of tents and way too many smells for it to be just a small troop. You know what that means."

"Fuck." Ira's tail slapped the ground. "How are we supposed to get to Georgia with a whole army between us?"

"We can't let that stop us. We have to get to her. Now," Ryu growled, smoke already puffing up his throat. Turning to their soldiers, Ryu waved an arm at them to get moving. "Let's move out. Don't make any sudden movements and stick to the tree line until we can find a safe time to infiltrate the camp site."

"Ryu!" Desmond stalked over to him, grabbing his arm before he could walk away. "This is suicide. You're going to get us all killed and for what? A human female that isn't worth all this effort."

Before he knew what he was doing, Ryu swung around and slammed his fist into Desmond's face. Grabbing him by the throat before he could fall, Ryu roared.

"I am your king. You will do as I command, or you can leave."

Desmond pushed against Ryu's hand, his claw digging in where Ryu held him. Ira placed a hand on Ryu's shoulder.

"Ryu, come on. You know I want to get her back as much as you do."

Ryu's hand tightened on Desmond's throat. A choking sound came from Desmond's throat before Ryu released him. Desmond stumbled back, rubbing his throat with his hand.

"He'd rather we leave her to them." Ryu gestured a hand at Desmond with a snarl. "He doesn't seem to understand the gravity of our situation."

Bent at the waist, his hands on his knees, Desmond choked out a laugh.

"I get it. I do. If she dies, we're one step closer to dying. I just don't think charging into a camp of what looks like close to ten thousand soldiers without the numbers to back us up." Desmond pushed himself up to a standing position. "Besides, I don't think you can do anything about it right now anyway. She's getting married."

Ryu's heart stuttered. "What?"

"Yeah, your precious princess was in the process of being married when we peeked into the camp." Desmond watched Ryu's face for his reaction. "I'm not sure that's a female who wants to be saved."

Jaw clenched, Ryu unsheathed his halberd and swung it with a yell at the nearest tree. The blade sunk halfway into the trunk of the tree. Ryu wiggled the handle until it came loose.

"There has to be a reason. There's no way she would have married him without a reason. Did you see anything else?"

"Depends, are you going to hit me again?" Desmond angled away from him.

Ryu blew out a long breath, staring down at the ground.

"No. I'm not going to hit you again. At least, not yet."

"We need to find a way to get close to Georgia without having to dive headfirst into a massive army." Ira's good eye glanced up at the sky while his claw scratched at his cheek.

"There's a carriage waiting on the end of the camp," Desmond offered. "Perhaps it is waiting for the happy couple," – Ryu growled – "to leave. We can wait until they're at the edge of the camp, and maybe we can cause a distraction while you grab her?"

"That's workable." Ira nodded. "Ryu?"

Ryu thought about it for a moment. It was true. They could get Georgia if they ambushed the carriage. Get to her without having to throw themselves into the middle of Callahan's army. However, that would mean...

"We'd have to wait until after she's married to get to her," Ryu stated with a resigned sigh.

Desmond's lips curled up on one side in a grimace. "Unfortunately."

Ryu pressed his lips together tightly. "Fine. Let's go."

They gathered up their troops and crept along the tree line just as Ryu had commanded before. It was a slow and tedious process. Especially since at that very moment, Georgia, his princess, was getting married to someone else.

It wasn't like Ryu expected her to marry him. The drakes didn't have a marriage ceremony in the way that the humans did. Most of their females were in relationships with multiple other males. They would have to have a marriage ritual for all of them and that seemed a bit ridiculous.

That didn't mean Ryu wanted Georgia to marry anyone else, either. The very thought of it made the beast inside of him want to cart her off and hide her away in the caves. Or maybe a castle. She'd probably prefer something that let her see the sky.

Thankfully, the carriage was parked near the edge of the woods. Ryu would have punished the guards, if they were his. Their lax security put them in a position to be ambushed so easily.

Ryu's head jerked at a round of cheers and clanging of metal, the ground rumbling with the massive amount of thumping at once. After a few moments, the crowd of soldiers shifted, splitting for the oncoming royals. Ryu caught a glimpse of long black hair and almost stepped out of the tree's shadows.

Ira placed a hand on his chest. "Patience, brother."

It took everything in Ryu to hold back as Georgia came into view with that monster of a man close at her side. The pinched expression on her face made a low rumble begin in his chest. There was no doubt in Ryu's mind that this marriage was not something Georgia wanted. Her father trailing behind them with Luis almost carrying him added further proof.

Ryu's very being vibrated with the need to move as they watched Callahan and Georgia climb into the carriage. The soldiers surrounded them moved back into the camp, leaving only a handful of them to guard the carriage.

"Now," Ira whispered in a sharp tone.

They took off in a blur of movement. The guards near the carriage barely saw the drakes coming as they fell upon the entourage. Ryu's blade slid into the first man with ease, while the butt of his halberd's pole smacked into the head of another coming from the side. The curtains of the carriage fluttered, and Georgia's lovely face peered out through the window before Callahan shoved her back into the carriage.

"Georgia!" Ryu pushed past the soldier to make his way to the carriage.

Callahan called out to the driver, and the driver flicked the reins, causing the horses to move forward.

"The horses!" Ira shouted to some of the drakes to get in the way. The horses didn't like the drakes being so close, and they reared up and neighed. No matter how much the driver smacked them, the horses refused to move forward.

A few feet from the carriage, Ryu came face to face with one of the humans Ryu wanted to see.

Luis.

The dark-haired prince was wiping blood off his blade, the king face down in the mud blood pooling around his neck.

Ryu bared his fangs at the dark-haired prince. "You. I'm going to enjoy killing you."

The Plumus prince smirked at him, unsheathing his sword, his other hand holding a dagger that seemed awfully familiar to Ryu.

"I haven't killed a drake yet, but you'll all be gone soon enough. Let's start with you."

Swinging his halberd, Ryu grunted as Luis caught it between his two blades. They struggled for a moment, as Ryu swiped out with his tail at a soldier coming at his side.

"Ryu!" Georgia called out with a pained grunt.

Ryu's head jerked to the side. It was enough of a distraction to give Luis an opening. Pain sliced through his arm. Ryu glared at Luis and charged at him.

We can't hold them and get her, Ira called to Ryu's. *The others will come any moment. What do you want to do?*

As if Ira talking about it caused it to happen, an alarm blared in the camp and the rumbling of foot falls vibrated the ground beneath them. Ryu glanced at the carriage and then to the army coming up on them.

Where's Desmond?

With a growl of frustration, Ryu swiped his halberd at Luis. He ducked, just as the drake king expected. That let Ryu smacked Luis in the chest so hard that it knocked the breath out of him.

Ira's answer came back a moment later. *I don't see him. He was heading for the carriage.*

Fuck.

If they left now, there would be nothing to show for it. This would have all been for nothing, and that did not sit well with Ryu. How would he explain to Aryn that he had Georgia within reach and wasn't able to get her back? They would be right back to where they started with no princess and a prince on his way to destroy them all.

Luis coughed and groaned, as an idea came to Ryu.

Ryu's lips curled in a snarl of fangs. "We're leaving. Everyone back to the trees." Before Luis could catch his breath completely, Ryu cracked the prince hard with the butt of his haberd. As Luis fell, Ryu wrapped his hand around his throat and jerked him forward. "You're coming with me."

Ryu threw the unconscious prince over his shoulder and glared over his shoulder back at the carriage.

Desmond. Come on!

There was no answer.

Ryu, we have to go. Ira shouted in his head now.

Desmond still hadn't answered or appeared by the carriage. Where had he gone? Maybe he'd already taken off into the woods? With the human army closing in on him, he didn't have time to look for him. He'd have to trust that Desmond could take care of himself.

With a reluctant growl, Ryu ran to catch up with his warriors.

This wasn't over. Ryu would get his princess back if he had to burn

down every castle in the kingdom
to get to her.

Epilogue
Cal

CAL WATCHED OVER the Kinoko royals and commoners alike from the top of the amphitheater. Flowers of all colors wrapped around the balconies and columns. Candles and artwork brought in of the king's likeness surrounded the stone altar in which they had laid out the dead king's body.

Draped in purple and black, the king's body showed through the sheer white fabric covering his head to the soles of his feet. The crowd was quiet in reverence to the late King of the Kinokos. For all his weakness and faults, Fergus had been beloved by his people.

The way they celebrated one's life in such an elaborate display made Cal's skin crawl. Death was not something to be celebrated. It was to be feared and threatened upon those who sought to defy him. His father had taught him that lesson well.

His hands tightened together before his waist as he watched his new bride slowly make her way to the front of the room. Dressed in black, Georgia wore a matching veil over her face, her hands clasping a bundle of white lily.

To the crowd, she was the mourning daughter. They didn't know that the reason she wore the veil was because of the punishment she had received on her arrival.

Cal licked the split of his lip where the princess and soon-to-be queen had bitten him upon their marriage. He hadn't believed the princess would come quietly. She hadn't been exactly compliant so far, but at least she had the decency to think of her kingdom's welfare over her own. Her time with the drakes had changed her.

If he hadn't witnessed it firsthand, Cal could see it in her eyes. The fire. No longer would she silently take what he dealt her. Even if he could get his brother back and get crowned as the reigning king, Cal knew Georgia would have to be dealt with.

But in time.

Sucking in a breath, Cal let it out slow and steady. The time would come. He couldn't get rid of her now. Not after Cal had just got her back.

The people had already lost their king. They needed time to mourn. Time to adjust to the new rule. Infiltrating a kingdom and usurping its king was all good and well in theory. However, people were far more likely to accept Cal as their ruler if he seemed as if he was their ally and not an enemy overthrowing their kingdom. Any other way would end with riots that would cost Cal more time, money, and bodies that he wanted to spend.

No, the 'barrel in and take everything' plan wasn't going to work anymore. Not now that he had to kill the Kinoko king to get what he wanted.

Cal's eyes lingered on the profile of Georgia's face. He knew a lingering purple and blue bruise covered the side of her cheek and eye. Such a pity to mess up such a pretty face. He would have avoided it had she been compliant with the wedding night.

As it were, without his brother, there it was more difficult to handle the princess than before. Especially with the new training she seemed to have obtained in her absence. Cal's hand slid up to the bandage of his healing side. He wouldn't underestimate her again.

"Your Highness."

Cal angled his head to the side before turning his eyes to the soldier waiting for him to continue.

"The drake."

Cal shot him a warning look.

"I mean, the prisoner." The soldier quickly corrected himself. "You wanted to know when he woke up again."

Lips curling up, Cal waved the soldier away before turning his gaze back to his new bride.

Georgia may have gained a few new tricks, but Cal had something in his pocket as well.

The drake king's brother.

Turning from the crowd, Cal made his way through the corridors and down the stairs. He accepted condolence for his loss from passing nobles with a tight polite smile, his hands behind his back.

No one knew what really happened to the Kinoko king. The story they spread painted the drakes as the culprits during an ambush in the camp. The Kinoko soldiers fought to get their beloved princess back, and their precious king threw himself in front of his daughter to save her from the brutish drakes.

At least that's the story they'd spun.

Cal doubted the people would be happy to know it was Cal's brother who had sliced their dear king's throat at their princess's wedding, no less.

Leaving the amphitheater, Cal climbed into a waiting carriage. He drew the curtains so he didn't have to bother pretending to be distraught about his father-in-law's demise.

If Cal had it his way, the Kinoko king would have died before he had even arrived. Not that the old man had done much to thwart Cal's plans. He didn't even know what kind of man he had brought in for his daughter to marry or that Cal and Lu had been playing with her.

If Cal hadn't come in to take over, someone else would have, and they would have razed the kingdom to the ground. Cal planned on bringing them into Plumus. No reason to waste good able-bodied workers.

The carriage came to a stop with a jerk. Cal grunted and glared at the driver on his way out. They would definitely have to be retrained. Things had become too lax, and Cal would tighten the reins now that he had control.

Instead of walking into the palace, Cal made a beeline for the gate house. He couldn't keep his prisoner where the other criminals were kept, after all.

Cal wouldn't let anyone ruin his fun. He needed an uninterrupted place to take care of his guest. Somewhere the guards still loyal to the princess wouldn't ask questions.

The old armory had been the perfect place to store his fire breathing guest. The stone walls kept the place from burning down around their ears as well as they kept the sounds from drawing in unwanted attention.

Cal stepped off the final step into the darkened room. Chains rattled, and a groan signaled that his guest was awake and ready for their next session.

Strolling further into the room, Cal lit a torch and brought it closer to the groaning drake's face. Metal chains locked legs and arms against the wall. They had to add an extra one for the tail. It had a mind of its own, swiping out to knock the guards off their feet.

At his presence, a low growl emanated from the prisoner.

Smirking at the sound, Cal brought the torch up to the drake's face tapping his fingers on the metal muzzle they had to fashion onto his face to keep him from burning them alive.

"Now, now. No need to get upset. We haven't even gotten started yet." Cal trailed his torch up and down the drake taking in his battered form, those golden eyes burning into him with so much hatred it made Cal burn with glee. "We're going to have so much fun together. Just you wait."

About the Author

Erin Bedford is an otaku, recovering coffee addict, and Legend of Zelda fanatic. Her brain is so full of stories that need to be told that she must get them out or explode into a million screaming chibis. Obsessed with fairy tales and bad boys, she hasn't found a story she can't twist to match her deviant mind full of innuendos, snarky humor, and dream guys.

On the outside, she's a work from home mom and bookbinger. One the inside, she's a thirteen-year-old boy screaming to get out and tell you the pervy joke they found online. As an ex-computer programmer, she dreams of one day combining her love for writing and college credits to make the ultimate video game!

Until then, when she's not writing, Erin is devouring as many books as possible on her quest to have the biggest book gut of all time. She's written over thirty books, ranging from paranormal romance, urban fantasy, and even scifi romance.

http://www.erinbedford.com